RED FROGS and other plays

THE ELEKTRA FUGUES,
RED FROGS and
STADIUM DEVILDARE

By

Ruth Margraff

NoPassport Press

Dreaming the Americas Series

RED FROGS and other plays by Ruth Margraff Copyright 2012.

The Elektra Fugues © 1996, 2012 by Ruth Margraff

Red Frogs © 2002, 2012 by Ruth Margraff

Stadium Devildare © 2005, 2012 by Ruth Margraff

All rights reserved. Except for brief passages quoted in newspaper, magazine, radio, or television reviews, no part of this book may be reproduced in any form or by any means, electronic or mechanical, without permission in writing from the author. Professionals and amateurs are herby warned that this material, being fully protected under the Copyright Laws of the United States of America and of all the other countries of the Berne and Universal Copyright Conventions, is subject to royalty. All rights including, but not limited to professional, amateur, recording, motion picture, recitation, lecturing, public reading, radio and television broadcasting, and the rights of translation into foreign languages are expressly reserved. Particular emphasis is placed on the question of readings and all uses of this play by educational institutions, permission for which must be secured from the author and publisher.

All performance queries, professional, stock and amateur, need be directed by contacting Ms. Margraff's agent Susan Schulman: A Literary Agency, 454 West 44th Street, NY, NY 10036. Phone: 212-713-1633. http://www.schulmanagency.com

Cover photo credit: Nina Hellman in *Red Frogs*, photography by Bob Handelman © bobhandelman.com

NoPassport Press Dreaming the Americas Series, First edition 2012 by NoPassport Press, PO Box 1786, South Gate, CA 90280 USA; e-mail: NoPassportPress@aol.com, website: www.nopassport.org. ISBN: 978-1-300-32500-0

RED FROGS and other plays

By
Ruth Margraff

Introduction by director **Tim Maner**
THE ELEKTRA FUGUES

Introduction by director **Elyse Singer**
RED FROGS

Introduction by co-directors **Richard Werner**
and **Karen Jean Martinsen**
STADIUM DEVILDARE

Afterword by **Randy Gener**

NoPassport Press

Dreaming the Americas Series

Line editors for this volume: Otis Ramsey-Zoe
and Caridad Svich

Introduction to THE ELEKTRA FUGUES

By Tim Maner

As you entered HERE Arts Center for the Tiny Mythic Theatre's performance of THE ELEKTRA FUGUES, Elektra, clad in black leather, was already talking to her father Agamemnon—a deus ex machina whose image shone from a TV inside a dark, silvery pedestal. Despite her punk clothing she was regressively supplicating, while his answers were pseudo-comforting and manipulative.

> "I'm starting to cry again, Daddy ... " /"You do that so I'll pick you up, to get my attention. ... "/ "But I love this story and I love you and I hate my mother." -Kyle Gann, Village Voice, December 31, 1996

Well, I love this story too and I was lucky enough to direct its first production. In the mid-90's, I was transitioning from being the co-artistic director of Tiny Mythic Theatre to co-director of a thriving new arts center in Soho called HERE. It was a very exciting and artistically vibrant time for me and, in my memory, for New York City as a whole. Of the myriad experiences and collaborations of that time, one which will always stand out for me was working with Ruth Margraff.

I first heard words written by Ruth when her play GAT HIM TO HIS PLACE (a biblical western from Judges 19, KJV) was presented in our summer American Living Room Festival. I knew immediately that I had to work with her. I asked for an introduction and that led eventually to our co-founding The Opera Project, a multi-year collaboration with Matthew Pierce (composer), Allen Hahn (set/light designer), Nancy Brous (costume designer), and Celise Kalke (dramaturg). THE ELEKTRA FUGUES was our first full-length collaboration.

In THE ELEKTRA FUGUES, Ruth has taken various recorded versions of the Electra story (Aeschylus, Sophocles, Euripides, etc.) and spliced them into an octet of voices through which she tells her story of family dysfunction. With these tracks—built like an obsolete 8-track recording—she riffs on the fugue as a musical form (polyphonic voices, thematic counterpoint) and as psychiatric state (memory and forgetting, actions without recollection). But, it's not the complex, intelligent construction and architecture that makes the piece. It's the strangely familiar family that Ruth created.

In casting this family, I turned Agamemnon (Richard Rose) into an electronic voice-over emitted ominously from a mortuary sort of obelisk. I cast two Meredith Monk-trained singers for the sisters: Mercedes Bahleda as

Cassandra, and Dina Emerson as Chrysothemis/Iphigenia. Dina's voice would erupt from a slit in her throat as if from a previous sister, a previous family disaster from which she thought she had long ago healed. I cast Justin Vivian Bond as Clytemnestra—a synthetically-gendered and silicone-injected step-mother figure. Thomas Pasley, as Aegisthus, was her guileful lounge lizard step-daddy side-kick. Eric Sanders played Orestes the bed-wetting militant poser with windblown rock n'roll hair. For our Peasant Husband/Gilbert Murray, tenor Tony Boutte became a revisionist historian inspired by an actual 1930s translator of Greek tragedies and the saccharine-sweet American films of his generation. I stood in as Tony's understudy a few times when he was called away. And finally, in Abigail Gampel's gravelly gutteral voice, I saw Elektra as an unceasing protester whose raging punk rants propel her family toward their ultimate and total destruction.

There had been a number of high-profile airplane crashes during the 1990s including the death of 7-year old pilot Jessica Dubroff and her pilot father who was training her, and the crash of TWA Flight 800 where the search for the black box recorder had made headlines. Ruth told me when she was writing the last scene of THE ELEKTRA FUGUES she ended up flying in a very small plane with her only copy of the play. She became terrified that she was going to crash, but was comforted by the thought that somehow her play would survive and that could serve as a black-box recording where she would have the chance to make one last statement. She eventually wrote this story into her last lines of the play: *"I found out later they don't put black box recorders on those single engine planes because they're too small. And at the time nobody that knew me even knew I was up in the air."*

I love how Ruth transformed that utterly intimate moment of her own fear of dying and being forgotten, into the final words that Elektra speaks. It reminds me of why I feel so connected to her writing. She blurs the personal and the mythological. She sees larger-than-life stories in terms that are life-sized and she gives mythic weight to the achingly personal.

Tim Maner created the lyrics, book, concept and additional music for LIZZIE BORDEN produced at the Living Theatre in 2009, named in The Advocate's "Top Ten of 2009" and nominated for three Drama Desk Awards. Tim has written, directed and produced over 20 original music/theater works including *The Opera Project*, a trilogy of new wave operas with writer Ruth Margraff. He is a founding member of the critically acclaimed Tiny Mythic Theatre Company and HERE Arts Center.

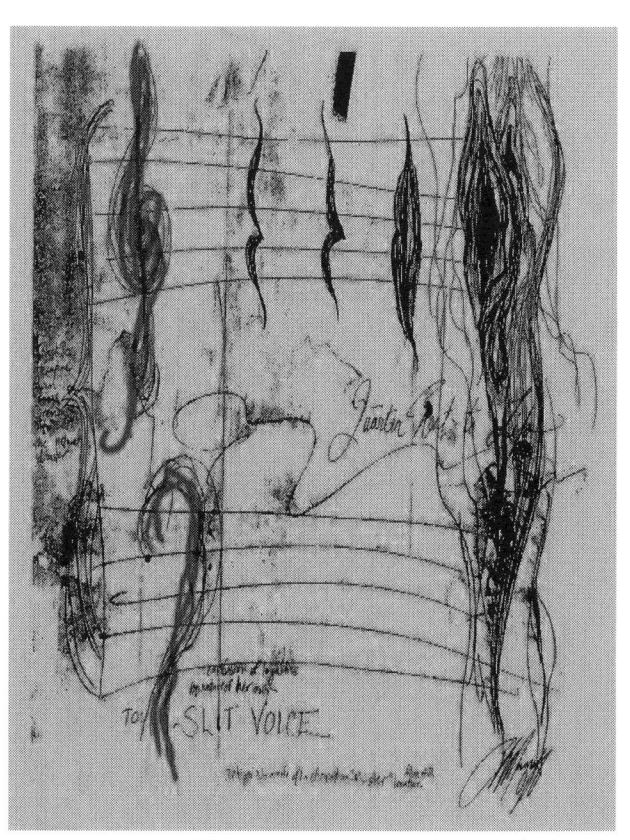

"Quarter Rest to Lip to Slit Voice" drawing by Ruth Margraff

THE ELEKTRA FUGUES
a black box recording of classic disaster

by

Ruth Margraff

THE ELEKTRA FUGUES was previously published in the anthology DIVINE FIRE: Eight Contemporary Playwrights Inspired by the Greeks from Backstage/Watson-Guptill Publications ©2005 ISBN: 0-8230-8851-0

This version of THE ELEKTRA FUGUES is copyrighted 2012. All rights reserved exclusively by Librettist.

Production History

THE ELEKTRA FUGUES was commissioned by HERE Arts Center's "Opera Project"/Tiny Mythic Theatre Company as an "8-track opera based in vocal cadence, punk & classic strings" and premiered as an opera November 26 - December 21, 1996. It was scored for a live 7-piece chamber orchestra of violin, viola, cello, upright bass, electric violin, guitar and percussion.

Director: Tim Maner

Composer: Matthew Pierce

Dramaturgy/Viola: Celise Kalke

Set & Lighting design: Allen Hahn

Costume design: Nancy Brous

Dina Emerson............Iphigenia/Chrysothemis

Tony Boutte/Tim Maner (understudy).......Peasant Husband

Abigail Gampel.......................Elektra

Eric Sanders............................Orestes

Mercedes Bahleda......................Cassandra

Thomas Pasley.........................Aegisthus

Justin Bond aka "Kiki".....................Clytemnestra

Richard Rose..............................Deus Ex Machina

Here Arts Center photos courtesy of NancyBrous.com

THE ELEKTRA FUGUES was also produced February 11 - March 13, 1999 *a capella,* as a play with one live percussionist by Bottom's Dream Theater in Los Angeles.

Director: Jim Martin

Alice Dodd...............................Elektra

Jennifer Griffin........................Clytemnestra

Cheryl White...................Iphigenia/Chrysothemis

Matthew Posey.......................Aegisthus

Mike Hagiwara..........................Orestes

William Mesnik.......................Peasant Husband

THE ELEKTRA FUGUES was developed with readings directed by Liz Diamond at the Lincoln Center Library reading series and New Dramatists in New York as well as a reading directed by Brad Rothbart at Theater Double in Philadelphia.

Special Thanks

To Caridad Svich and the beloved HERE opera project members Tim Maner, Celise Kalke, Matthew Pierce, Allen Hahn & Nancy Brous; to Mitchell Gossett and Jim Martin of Bottom's Dream, Vicky Boone/Frontera@Hyde Park Theater & Jason Neulander/Salvage Vanguard for hosting me with a Laurie Carlos NEA residency in Austin, Texas during the summer I wrote most of this, Meredith Monk via Dina Emerson, Greil Marcus, Gilbert Murray, Herb Dishman of Fairy Stain/Engine Run Angry and his single engine plane, Joe Ridout, Douglas Greene, Eric Sanders, Phyllis Slattery, Audrey Parks, my mother & her apartment by the carbon-monoxide Queens Tunnel, McKnight Foundation, The Playwrights' Center, RAT Conference in Austin and the wrath of the homeless teenage girls I worked with through choreographer Margery Segal.

Roles: *Vocal Cadence of Archetypes*

ELEKTRA

[punk/rage]

CHRYSOTHEMIS/IPHIGENIA

[sister sweet to slit voice]

CLYTEMNESTRA

[stand-up comedic whine of synthetic breastmilk]

AEGISTHUS

[stand-up comedic whine of stepfather guile]

ORESTES

[militant/percussive/bedwetting]

PEASANT HUSBAND/GILBERT MURRAY

[preface of a mild translation]

DEUS EX MACHINA

[Agamemnon, can be pre-recorded]

Sequence

Act I. TRANSMISSION OF OLD GLEAM

Scene 1: "**Obelisk**"—Elektra at the deus ex machina crash site, with Iphigenia's **"Pity Me Father."** Scene 2: "**Resemble Overture**" a fugue of family portraits, pitched in reaction to Elektra's lament

Act II. ELEKTRA'S RANT

Scene 1: **"Like a Dog"**—the tonal centre of the fugues with "**A Little For Your Easing**." Scene 2: "**Not Fraught With Toil**"

Act III. SHUT UP

Scene 1: "**Sister**"—Elektra tries to enlist Chysothemis, a sister who has sprung up in the sister position of Iphigenia from a more psychological translation. Scene 2: "**Clytemnestra's Countour I**"

Act IV. RECOGNITIONS OF THE BROTHER

Scene 1: "**Signet Ring**." Scene 2: "**Scar on his Brow**." Scene 3: "**Gleaming Lock of Curls**" with "**Muscular Footprint**" duets. Scene 4: "**Urn**" into "**Final Girl Staircases**." Scene 5: "**Clytemnestra's Contour II**;" Scene 6: "**God's Horseman And A Star Without A Stain**"

Act V. RED PILLARS

Scene 1: "**Parlour**"—To carry out the dreadful shape. Scene 2: "**Lay Clean the Flank**." Scene 3: "**Cost of Driving**." Scene 4: "**Flotsam Oracle**." Scene 5: "**Blood Songs**", furies in adjustment to the overwhelming unison of fugues

Act VI. GIRL-LIKE FACE

Scene 1: **"Deus Ex Machina"** an inversion to disembodied girlness, still unmated and untranslated by the father of straight children, nowhere to be found, as he could no longer maintain an erection in the noise. Scene 2: **"Slit Voice"** and Scene 3: "**Black Box Recording**"

Abigail Gampel as Elektra (Here Arts Ctr, NYC)

Act I. TRANSMISSION OF OLD GLEAM

Scene 1: "Obelisk"

ELEKTRA at the crash site of AGAMEMNON'S grave, is illuminated by erupting gleams as if watching an old home movie that no longer exists.

ELEKTRA: What were we doing in the woods…

DEUS EX MACHINA: That's where we lived, that was our home

ELEKTRA: But we didn't have walls on our house

DEUS EX MACHINA: We were free to frolic and run all over through the trees which are the only walls the gods make—in the blazing daylight—we were blurry… wild…creatures

ELEKTRA: And the golden brother…on a rocking horse with his gleaming lock of curls?…was he eating anything?

DEUS EX MACHINA: Maybe leaves, maybe some flowers

ELEKTRA: Did you see the daugthers both at first sight or not really

DEUS EX MACHINA: I was deep in thought…but the goddess saw me the whole time, she was waiting for me but I want you to think about things deeply, they'll be trying to distract you

ELEKTRA: But I love this story (and I love you and I hate my mother). And then what did you have to shoot her with?

DEUS EX MACHINA: An arrow probably, it's all a blur now, it was a response honey the way we fight a battle to adjust to something that has pissed us off, it is involuntary, just like things were blurry right before I taught you how to talk and taught you the names of all the birds, even the bird you hated immediately

ELEKTRA: Is that the sister who keeps shining

Gleam of IPHIGENIA/CHRYSOTHEMIS, who starts to sing

DEUS EX MACHINA: That's her music. It may not be sweet or joyful but it's a very old gleam and you know you used to sound crazy too when you were small but now you can talk to me

ELEKTRA: I'll remember it. *[rote]* I hate my mother because she tricked you and tricked the wild creature into scaring you and startling the wild creature and the bullet came whirling out of that

DEUS EX MACHINA: I'll tell you what to do

ELEKTRA: Exactly what to do

DEUS EX MACHINA: I'll carry you in my everlasting arms and hold you like this 'til you're older and it starts to get clear.

ELEKTRA: But I'm starting to cry again Daddy, I can't stop crying anymore

DEUS EX MACHINA: You do that so I'll pick you up, to get my attention

ELEKTRA: No because it's so sad. It's sad how we waited for your footsteps and the creature how she thought she would look beautiful dying and wide-eyed. Somebody's throat everybody wants to slit. She was more appealing as a sacrifice. I'd probably just sleep until my muscle tissue rebuilt itself. I'd probably just stop in my tracks. Or maybe turn a little towards the arrow, Open up my neck so the curls fall back from my throat and hear the twig snap underneath your foot and maybe it's the beast with the teeth and claws or maybe it's Daddy. But at least I would be injured finally so I'd have an injury and not just sadness, something that would heal over and be mine.

IPHIGENIA: Pity me Father

DEUS EX MACHINA: Honey I can't hear you very well

Gleam from the DEUS EX MACHINA briefly illuminates ORESTES, who is holding his sword.

ORESTES: Don't forget about his hands, how he can toss you high up in the air above his head and fly you like that, don't forget you were his little airplane too, just like me.

ELEKTRA: You're listening to her now aren't you, it's her turn already and you do pity her

IPHIGENIA: Pity me Father

DEUS EX MACHINA: Honey I don't understand why you're still crying. Maybe when you learn how to talk you can tell me what it's all about. Crazy little girl.

IPHIGENIA: Is it all forgot

ELEKTRA: She's stainless isn't she so you can choose to stain her, punish her. But I'm the one still singing all your praises, I know them all by heart. Old Gleam Not Unto Joy Nor Sweet—

DEUS EX MACHINA: Yes. Oh yes the cadence. Not unto joy nor sweet music nor shining of gold...*[trails off, deep in thought]*

"Pity Me Father"

IPHIGENIA: *Pity me Father*

Is it all forgot

How often in your feasting

Rang my sweet strains

When I, a stainless girl sang pure

Sang of my sire, sang gifts and heaven to you

Falling so fragile, pity me Father

Is it all forgot

Say grace

Say grace

Act I, Scene 2: "Resemble Overture"

A Familial Fugue of Portrait Features and Archetypal Pitches:

ORESTES	IPHIGENIA	AEGISTHUS	[cont'd]
[militant] We shudder to think of death's cold terrors. We believe that we are plural.	*[final girl]* Run run run for your life!	*[stand up]* So there's this doctah, he says to the lady, "Is your hubby naggin you about them saggy baggy boobs, uh lemme see what I can do for yah knockahs. Just don't go pickin up the luggage or you'll hear a sorta rippin and you'll get all sticky." So she gets the augmentation she says "I don't feel a thing now when you feel me up and	put me under, every time I'm strippin, hell, my booby slides around there to my backside, what did you do to me?" And I said "honey, you come back to surgery, I musta put a ping pong ball in there by mistake" she says "Doc, I'm gonna sue you. I paid you to take this grapefruit offa my ovary
We pray the day will someday shine when we lead a useful life without this ammunition.	The staircases are edited together!		
	The stairway is the other way!		
	The staircase winding?		
But please God save our muscles!	Falling flat?		
	Coming from inside the house-		

PEASANT HUSBAND [softshoe]	IPHIGENIA [final girl/horror movie-like]	CLYTEM-NESTRA [stand up]	[cont'd] a knot when you were in the state of gristle.
How you were shattered by a shock too terrible,	Run run run for your life!	Honey no I know you loathe me and you loathe yourself but gimme somethin on the rocks you know I'm all choked up! You pay some rent or I'll have you lobotomized. Y'sound like a hemorrhage and frankly, I've had better hemorrhages. Oh God I shoulda pumped my breast, drank my own milk and scoffed at you screaming, tied your chords in	I shoulda knocked out every tooth as soon as it came in. Should've beaten you for every frown,
You were wild,	Run run run for your life!		
An experience too damaging,	The staircases are edited together!		I should've snapped your spine like the twig you were!
Too shattering,	Get away from there boy, better watch your back! The stairway is the other way! The staircase winding?		
Too shocking for a girl to bear,			
Too terrible for a girl,			Oh lookat that I spilled the soft drink oh it woulda been so soft
What's a girl to do,	Coming from inside the house!		
To bear—			
	Coming from inside the house!		

20 ~ *The Elektra Fugues*

Act II, ELEKTRA'S RANT

Scene 1: "Like a Dog"

ELEKTRA'S punk rock rant in reaction to overture, a lament to her sire, which the PEASANT HUSBAND tries to translate for himself from the glow of his sweetly burning lamp, beside his reading chair. Intermitantly, IPHIGENIA echoes ELEKTRA's lament in a treble descant.

/ = overlapping argument, interrupting each other

ELEKTRA: *LIKE A DOG I SERVE. I TOIL. I HEED THE DREADFUL/ CAUSE.*

PEASANT HUSBAND: Beneath this sweetly burning lamp I think of what I know. I know I / want you.

ELEKTRA: *LIKE A WORM I PINE. I GNASH. I WASTE AWAY MY PRIME, I WRECK MY LOVELINESS, I CHOKE MY SWEETNESS, I REEK LIKE SWEAT, I HOPE I VEX YOU, BEG YOU, WALLOW YOU. I SERVE YOU AND I TOIL. I DREAD, I CURSE. I'M BENDING OVER BACKWARDS MOTHERFUCKING-FUCK ME, WHORE ME, SLAVE ME, CAST ME OUT AND FLAY ME, PAY ME NOTHING. SO I SUCKLE AT YOUR STASH SOME MORE. TICKLE UP YOUR FANCY LIZARD SPEWING YOU. AND SUCKIN ON YOUR SLUTNESS SORE. YEAH YOU RECKON ME MY GOLD. YOU RECKON ME MY SPOIL. YOU RECKON ME MY / BEAT AS THE DANCERS SWAY* [hey].

PEASANT HUSBAND: I can't remember learning how to read and yet a woman's mind so turns as easily as mine does. Just to see you better from this chair

ELEKTRA: *YOU ROTTEN RODENT ABJECT DASTARD MOTHERFUCKER, FUCK'ER HARDER, FUCK'ER DEEPER DIRTY.*

[*bittersweet*]: How the crying water

Wan lament of tears

And the cold blood lapping

At my sire's head

PEASANT HUSBAND: I am groomed and tailored with a small black hard rubber comb which I rinse after parting my hair. I can offer all / of this to you.

ELEKTRA: Drooped in the bed of slaughter, I'm the daughter. Drooped in the swell of slaughter, I'm the beggar, I'm the slave, I'm the roach. *SET FREE MY BROW. SET FREE MY BEGGAR BROW. AND RECKON ME MY SPOIL, FRAUGHT WITH TOIL. I BEWAIL, LAMENT MY SIRE* / But I'd never shrill a tear for you. I don't resemble you

PEASANT HUSBAND: I can provide the summer leisure to begin my scrutiny of you. How I'd love to have a famous wife and yet still find you barefoot in a summer dress / above the sink as a lark really

ELEKTRA [*tearing out her hair*]: LOOK AT THIS DEAD-LOCKED RAVAGED HAIR, IF I WAS YOU I'D TOIL TO BE FAIR, I'D LANGUISH IN THE LOOKING GLASS, COMBING IT UNTIL IT'S GOLD. THIS WHOLE FAMILY'S BLEACHED AND BLAZED AND BUTTERED [BUT ORESTES IS REALLY BLOND AND YOU FUCKING HATE THAT]! HOW YOU SPEND A FORTUNE GETTING IT TO SHIMMER TRESS BY TRESS INTO YOUR TREASON, WHATCHA GONNA DO WITH ALL THAT GLADNESS WHEN THE WAR'S NOT GOIN WELL FOR DADDY? HOW YOU GONNA SWIFT—CLOUD UP YOUR EYE WHEN HE COMES HOME?

[*rending her clothes*]

WHERE'S MY SATIN, SILK AND TANGLED SPOIL SPEWING IN YOUR THROBBING CUNT WITH DADDY'S BLACK BLOOD LAPPING AT THE BED?

DROOPED IN THE SWELL OF SLAUGHTER, I'M THE DAUGHTER, I'M THE BEGGAR, I'M THE ROACH, SET LOOSE MY DOGS.

PEASANT HUSBAND: Rinsing off something we've been growing in the yard

and feeding it to me and settling down,

children on the way.

We'll keep their school pictures on the mantle two years apart

PEASANT HUSBAND: I want to marry you a little for your easing. I can see clear through your dress.

23

ELEKTRA: *YOU HAVE MADE MY SIRE NAUGHT! YOU HAVE MADE ORESTES NAUGHT! And if I do resemble —*

[hesitation, "key" change to shrill]

NEVER MAY I RESPITE

NEVER MAY I CEASE FROM SORE LAMENT

NEVER MAY I LANGUISH

NEVER MAY I CURB THE FRENZIED PLAINT

NEVER MAY THE SPLENDOR

NEVER MAY I CLING TO SELFISH EASE

AND IF LIKE A DOG I SERVE

AND IF LIKE A WORM I TOIL

AND IF I DO RESEMBLE YOU —

[fatigue of terror to paralysis]

PEASANT HUSBAND: Preface of a mild translation.

CHORUS: And if I do. Resemble you. *(REPEAT)*

ELEKTRA: And if I do resemble you...

PEASANT HUSBAND: We'll do it all over in technicolor, I know it seems a little black and white for now but that's how I've been reading you beside this dim-watt bulb...

Act II, Scene 1:

"Not Fraught With Toil"

CLYTEMNESTRA and AEGISTHUS mock ELEKTRA's tantrums recklessly with CLYTEMNESTRA's narcotic ironies. AEGISTHUS treats ELEKTRA like a rabid, mangy dog due to his chronic hangovers. CLTEMNESTRA vomits a beautiful shining silver puddle, and uses it for a mirror.

CLYTEMNESTRA: Justice...slew your father

ELEKTRA: Under what law? Father be near—

CLYTEMNESTRA: If I could unfold ....my whole thought to the light...

ELEKTRA: A lover weighs more than a child in any woman's breast

Gleam of ORESTES laying a lock of his childhood curls on the DEUS EX MACHINA. CHRYSOTHEMIS appears and hides curls in her bosom.

DEUS EX MACHINA: Clear with the clear beams of the morrow's sun and it said to go to Troy. "Go forth to Troy" and who on earth has the bliss of heaven.

Alice Dodd as Elektra, Cheryl White as Chrysothemis
(Bottom's Dream Theater, LA)

Act III, SHUT UP

Two sisters spar for survival. CHRYSOTHEMIS reveals alliance with her mother at the very moment ELEKTRA tries to enlist her help in a blood vendetta.

CHRYSOTHEMIS: I'm your sister.

ELEKTRA: I don't believe I won't be terminated—

CHRYSOTHEMIS: I'm your sister.

ELEKTRA: If I cooperate—

CHRYSOTHEMIS: Come dear sister, I am not your foe but it's about your foe…your dreary wrath / and your profanity is, oh dear, it's loud. I overheard, I said I overheard them say

ELEKTRA: I don't know you or your happy-go-lucky malarkey politics

CHRYSOTHEMIS: They say you better bend before the strong, you better shorten your sails, better look a little harmless…/ if you don't shut up, well don't blame me if you can't turn to—

ELEKTRA: My father is dead. My sister's dead. My brother's probably dead.

CHRYSOTHEMIS: No he isn't—see and that is the terrific news. I was here this morning at the cemetery and somebody left this gleaming lock of curls on my father's grave.

DEUS EX MACHINA: It's kind of like... it's like I moved...out of my head...which is why you hear this echo darling, and you see all the way down to the wires

ELEKTRA: They killed my sister and they killed my father... This is my father's grave

CHRYSOTHEMIS: And he was my father.

ELEKTRA: This is holy ground.

CHRYSOTHEMIS: It's been hard on all of us.

ELEKTRA: You have no right to transgress holy ground—

CHRYSOTHEMIS: Maybe I should spend more time at the cemetery

ELEKTRA: Get off the ground

CHRYSOTHEMIS: Maybe I should holler and bellow at the top of my lungs the way you do

ELEKTRA: Get off

CHRYSOTHEMIS: On the other hand I'm getting by, I carry on.

ELEKTRA: Get away from me

CHRYSOTHEMIS: I sort of bend before the hateful.

ELEKTRA: Get lost!

CHRYSOTHEMIS: I mean I do run errands for the sake of the stepfamily. Which is probably compromising but I am entitled to my own adjustment!

ELEKTRA: Get out of here!

CHRYSOTHEMIS: You're not the only one in this family!

ELEKTRA: This is where they quenched my father, mangled him and cleft his soul, my father slew his thousands

CHRYSOTHEMIS: They say there's no turning back but you could turn back now...I'm telling you they're gonna kill you if you don't—I hope nobody saw me come here.

ORESTES: [*appearing with the flash of an urn*] Orestes is dead! and in this tiny urn. We'll bring the scanty relics home. I know you are thinking immediately of your dear Orestes, imagining him at his liveliest.

ELEKTRA: I'm not doing very well.

CHRYSOTHEMIS: They told me not to tell so don't tell anybody, but I feel like I can tell you...as somebody I can turn to—

ELEKTRA: Where do you turn—

CHRYSOTHEMIS: Turn to me

ELEKTRA: When you've got nowhere to go

CHRYSOTHEMIS [*leaning closer, as if to tell her the secret she has been holding back, she suddenly resembles Iphigenia*] Lying next to you for years in the shared room, our necks were parallel, our throats were quiet all those nights when they'd come bending down to kiss us both goodnight in the slant of light from the doorway—

ELEKTRA: When it's dark and you feel so blue.

CHRYSOTHEMIS: Daddy slipped and caught me by the neck but that was random...we were so very close in age—

ELEKTRA: I wanted to ask you something but I—

CHRYSOTHEMIS: They say like sisters and we were—

ELEKTRA: I know you'll think it's...no, no just forget it.

CHRYSOTHEMIS: You can't change what we are, Elektra

ELEKTRA: Oh God! No, Shut up! No.

CHRYSOTHEMIS: You shut up, I'm entitled to my own adjustment!

ELEKTRA & CHRYSOTHEMIS: *SHUT UP! SHUT UP! SHUT UP! SHUT UP! SHUT UP! SHUT UP! SHUT UP! SHUT UP! SHUT UP! SHUT UP! SHUT UP! SHUT UP! SHUT UP! SHUT UP!*

CHRYSOTHEMIS: No you shut up, shut up you're not the only one in this family. Shut up!

ELEKTRA: Oh God she mocks me. Shut up!

CHRYSOTHEMIS turns away.

CHRYSOTHEMIS: And if they told me anything it would be just like telling mother when it used to be the same as telling you because we told each other everything

ELEKTRA: Oh God who told her that?

CHRYSOTHEMIS: Just between you and me

ELEKTRA: Who does she believe?

CHRYSOTHEMIS: I hope nobody heard what I just said. I'll go forth upon my errand.

cast of The Elektra Fugues at Bottom's Dream Theater, LA

Act III, Scene 2

"Clytemnestra's Contour I"

CLYTEMNESTRA interrupts the argument, as if she has just unwittingly spawned CHRYSOTHEMIS as another ghastly offspring.

CLYTEMNESTRA: How nice to see the two of you getting along. *[a threat]* What are we chattering about to day girl friends. Oh god the poor girl has no breasts which one of them was it, or did I get them from a test tube. Answer me. I can't remember. Is it the younger one or not. The one standing slightly behind the other...foreground.. hm, in life span? Size of..? So you both got taller, get up and go to school...daddy's coloring ah hah well that's between the lines, eenie meany... Count to ten I'll suckle your milk, see how you feel. Kidding! Kids! Do not believe your ears. I thought I had a boy, what happened to him when he played with matches, guns and jagged objects, told him not to run so fast, stay out of the traffic. I'll get you implants when you graduate, both of you. I can't tell you apart when you stand that close together. How can I play favorites when I'm seeing double are you twins, answer me or I'll start menstruating backwards, are we regular, girls, what else is there to tell each other but we all have wombs, is there a problem here. I'm telling you Why whisper? It's your father tapping all the phones and shuddering the chandeliers. Does that make you wonder, well I wonder where all the hunters are today.

CLYTEMNESTRA figures out which of them is IPHIGENIA, her favorite, when she cries in her slit voice so she turns all her attention there. IPHIGENIA lays her throat bare walking toward her mother as if these are her very first steps.

CLYTEMNESTRA *[cooing]:* Oh come-mere. Come-mon. Come-mon you little swee-heart. Yea-ah you little swee-heart. Here she yis, Here she yis, Yeah I gotcha, Yea-ah, You a little swee-heart yea-ah, You just a little swee-heart sweet-as sugar *[IPHIGENIA starts to cry, can't see where she's going, bleeds from her slit throat]* Don'tcha cry oh don'tcha cry you break my heart you little swee-heart

IPHIGENIA: Mommy I don't feel good

CLYTEMNESTRA: That's because of all the evil people sweetie, you'd never believe what happens out there on the planet

IPHIGENIA: Was I bad?

CLYTEMNESTRA: Oh honey no, you were so perfect. You were the most perfect little slip of a girl with the sweetest little voice. I loved you all the time, I carried you. You were a bundle of pure joy and your little face just shined up at me like a little sunshine

IPHIGENIA: That's because I love you, mommy, and I draw you all those pictures of you and me and pick you all the flowers that blow... over the foothills...

IPHIGENIA makes it all the way to her mother's breast. They recline, sighing as IPHIGENIA drinks, and CLYTEMNESTRA looks gorgeous.

CLYTEMNESTRA: I hope you're not picking the flowers from your grave or your daddy's grave you never really know what's underneath those contours when they look like hills. I didn't know when I was pregnant for you that I would have another little girl but this one would be soft to me. This would be the little sweetheart and I'd never want to see her crying, I'd buy all the cushions in the kingdom for my little baby.

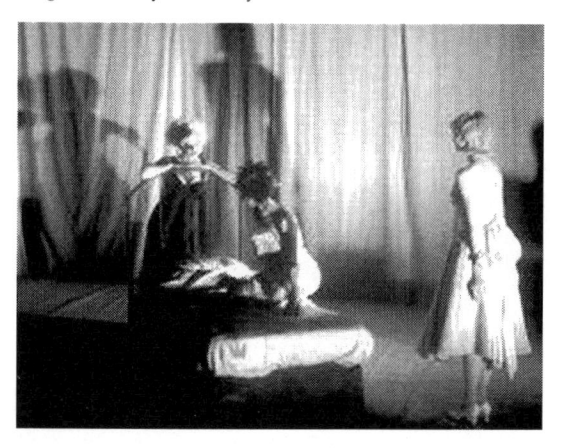

The Elektra Fugues directed by Jim Martin (Bottom's Dream Theater, LA)

Act IV. RECOGNITION OF THE BROTHER

Scene 1: "Signet Ring"

ORESTES disguised as messenger collapses from running for days and nights to get home

ORESTES: Orestes is dead!

Stylized gasping from ELEKTRA

IPHIGENIA *[as if subtitling silent film]:* Elektra mourns a golden boy. Attracting gleam of signet ring.

Act IV, Scene 2:

"Scar On His Brow"

ORESTES: *[as if stalking ELEKTRA]* Where do you live, where do you work, don't turn around, run away, what are you doing, do you see me, are you watching every move I make? Are you busy? Are you busy? Are you in a hurry? I gotta tell you something—

All tracks open: Furies

Orestes is dead.

Looming toward ELEKTRA.

DEUS EX MACHINA: *[slow bass voiceover]*: And who with the might of spear. And who with hand upon the hilt

IPHIGENIA: Elektra laments her brother's death but notices a scar on the messenger's brow.

Startle. ELEKTRA screams when ORESTES touches her, fights him; he appears to easily die. She gasps.

Act IV, Scene 3

"Gleaming Lock of Curls"

ORESTES adjusts. ELEKTRA relaxes and they listen to early punk music.

PEASANT HUSBAND *["footnote"]*: Golly gee, gee whiz. Some fellow oughtta spend a little money on the central figure of the tragedy. She might like icecream and perhaps the best abused of ancient tragedies, Oh darling, you're the counterrevolution of conventional classicism, but you could pretend to marry me.

ORESTES: Hey.

PEASANT HUSBAND: No one will know unless I tell them what your name means. I'll translate everything else into Rhyming English Verse.

ELEKTRA: Hey.

ORESTES: Yeah

ELEKTRA: What happened to your eye?

IPHIGENIA: I'm telling you he's following you…

ORESTES: So you know how, like you said the death of the planet was your masterpiece, how you were all about the bloodlust, I was varsity and you were distracted that if hey, if I smell like cigarettes it doesn't mean I'm drinking but I happen to be drinking, I get in a fight, I get a black eye but I also have a / good eye.

IPHIGENIA: ...following you home...

ORESTES: And *[deep voice]* "that's why I'm gonna kill you" —I just say that on my t-shirt I don't really mean it, people read into it if they read the liner notes and that's what rock n'roll is calling you to do

ELEKTRA: Unless we get along too well, even in the dark, it separates from your head / Like a haircut..

IPHIGENIA:...like the brother...

ORESTES: I told you what I'm doing is I'm moving. You will feel that, you'll look down at yourself and think about it later how I'm with you, maybe I am / somehow in you

IPHIGENIA: ...somehow...

ELEKTRA: Yeah

IPHIGENIA: And you think that it's the brother, maybe it's the brother.

ORESTES: I am present at this time and there is no mistake

ELEKTRA: What we were doing all those days we spent—

PEASANT HUSBAND: I can see clear through your dress. I'll take you on vacation to the sea. I can't remember learning how to read...

ORESTES: Five Million Years To Earth and these amplified, seamless teenage nights. One day it's boring and you hate it and the next day you have to stand in line to get a ticket and I miss the friendship, I miss the wrath, I mean at home he was a tourist, look at me...

PEASANT HUSBAND: I rinse the comb, I part my hair. I want to marry you a little for your easing

ELEKTRA: Devil take the rest of them

ORESTES: Here we go back to the chaos but for godsake here we go. Maybe it's a bad situation

ELEKTRA: Yeah

ORESTES: And maybe it's like really the fucking best.

ELEKTRA: In my ear....

PEASANT HUSBAND: I'll never rape you when I turn out the lamp. I'll leave it sweetly burning in the window. I'll fold the clothes when we take them off. I'll make up the bed every day. I'll marry you.

ORESTES: Hopefully landing very closely to your ear...drum...

PEASANT HUSBAND: I'll marry you a little for your easing.

ELEKTRA: What if we....get each other sick or the tracks touch down, get parallel, trains get scheduled

ORESTES: What if the whole thing's rotten in the heat, crash and burn, curse and regret and whatchagonna do about the blackmail by utility? I have no idea what Dad tried to tell me but I swear to God his lips were / moving

DEUS EX MACHINA: You are god's horse

ORESTES: You hear the voices and you're fucked. Actually you get some time because you hear the voices and you get a little grace period where you try to pretend you're doing really great and don't hear voices until one day some slip of the tongue *[outburst of dying words, panic]* I gotta lump in my throat!

ELEKTRA: What did Orestes die of *[choked up]*

ORESTES: It was a really long footrace, I don't think he had the training *[choked up]*

ELEKTRA: That's funny because we found a muscular footprint on the ground. It sort of looked like mine, I think it would be nice to see him again. *[choked up]*

ORESTES: Maybe he left it there a long time ago

ELEKTRA: Where was my brother. When it happened—

"Muscular Footprints" [duet]

CHRYSOTHEMIS:	PEASANT HUSBAND:
As if the gleaming footprint	Olderfashioned than we thought my dear, Twin beds we make as soon as we awaken
As if the gleaming heel	
As if the muscle of the footprint	Rinsing something we've been growing in the yard— and yet a woman's mind so turns as easily as mine does—
As if the curving arch	
As if to scan the track	We'll keep the Christmases
And frame and muscle	And holidays
Of the footprint	And birthdays
Safe deposits	Safe deposits
Increments of day	Increments of day
And savings	And savings
And we'll stay and stay	And we'll stay and stay

ELEKTRA: What did they do… with my brother's body.

ORESTES: They quickly burned his body on a pyre.

ORESTES sets an urn down in front of ELEKTRA and leaves her.

Act IV, Scene 4:

"Urn"

ELEKTRA: Orestes. Oh my God Orestes. Oh I grieve you baby, rock & roll bedwetter on your rocking horse an look at the horsey pee and see the horsey's leg fall off, it's empty in the socket, it was born dead, like you, you're a kid, you'll never grow up. Yeah you WEAR the Bad Black t-shirt little punk but you don't know black, I can show you fucking black, I'll cry you blackly, I can grieve your incapacity to show the fuck up. Pussy getting killed what? Runnin? Away from home was my idea. Think up your own grand exodus. You think you know what it's like to lose your shit, you never lost your shit we treated you like a china doll and you fucking played me. You hide the table knives or what? Did I scare you to death? Like I can't snap anybody's neck myself, like I need your fucking grip on the handle? What were you gonna do—roll in here in a smoke machine so you can freak them out with a couple of choked barchords, so they can say oh God you look just like your Daddy when you're butchered. Why didn't you tell me you weren't gonna MAKE IT back. There's no relief of pressure in my skull, it's way too hard to wait and fucking wait here like an idiot for you, and then to watch you goin dark. Oh God Orestes, you get sucked down in the masculine divine surveillance absence just like everybody else I touch and I just wanted you to be here watchin ME go dark, I'm goin down now, all the way, I see us both die clear as hell and I don't wanta do it by myself and I don't wanta do it, I don't wanta do it, I don't wanta do this but I gotta get the fuck away from Mom cause she's in charge of me. My head…..oh God my head…

"Final Girl Staircases"

IPHIGENIA

Run Run Run for your life! The staircases are edited together! The footstep creaking! On the stairwell stair! The staircase winding! Falling flat! Coming from inside the house is steepening! Get away from there, better watch your back!

ELEKTRA: It's too....

The stairway is the other way! The dog? The noise? The creepy music?

Landing at the landing!

Once she had descended dressed to the nines! She cried once on the barren ground! Cried like a faucet! She decided to go upstairs! To the swift! To the purple! To the hilt! As the sparks fly upward! And all the gashes look a little bit like mouths! All the gashes look a little bit like mouths!

It's too hard for you....

Act IV, Scene 5:

"Clytemnestra's Contour II"

CLYTEMNESTRA's outburst when she sees ORESTES in the house, and hears suspicious gasping from ELEKTRA.

CLYTEMNESTRA: So who was that the local / greyhound,

AEGISTHUS: Local vandal maybe, "have-not"

CLYTEMNESTRA: Yeah what's in the package there a pipe bomb / little jacknifes in the back?

AEGISTHUS: It's gonna trickle down there any day to skid row

CLYTEMNESTRA: Well I hope it's good news or we might get mad and kill the paper boy. I think we paid the bill so what's the problem / oh for god's sake get off of me

AEGISTHUS: Honey you're boobs are stickin out

CLYTEMNESTRA: What's so funny did he have his pants down / why do I always miss the private parts.

AEGISTHUS: You got a rupture in your boob, you got goo all over that nice blouse— / it's like super glue or something hold up a truck with that

CLYTEMNESTRA: Come 'ere paper boy I'll muster up a / fever for ya—

AEGISTHUS: Getta a pair of tongs on that / goo— see if it's cohesive

CLYTEMNESTRA: I'm down to 2 packs a day just so you know. / I feel like a new born baby!

CLYTEMN:
You're a billion years too late, you big bafoon, you're way off

Yeah how do you know it's me, it's prob'ly something you excreted—

God I go in spurts, sometimes I go crazy lustin for this reptile, other times I'm just crazy, Stop me! If I'm repeating myself

AEGISTHUS:
Nobody knows what the hell you're talking about, I gotta you know, leave the bedroom one of these days—

she's like a great big wad of gum and I got no teeth!

Toothless. Not a tooth in my head.

Stop her if she doesn't, she's a genius

CLYTEMNESTRA: What was the disaster, honey, What?

IPHIGENIA: Orestes is dead! *[three gasps]*

ELEKTRA: Orestes is dead. *[three gasps]*

CLYTEMNESTRA: *[Copy of the gasp, They all gasp]* Oh it could be worse. That little bed wetter...

AEGISTHUS: Save your quarters

CLYTEMNESTRA: I told him I was gonna put a clothespin on his dick but now they say that's bad psychology. He should've buckled down. Gone to the Olympics.

Thomas Pasley and Justin Bond (Here Arts Ctr, NYC)

Act IV, Scene 6:

"God's Horseman And A Star Without A Stain"

ORESTES' thinly veiled Olympic messenger display of Triumph, full-throttle, stadium rock.

ORESTES: I RAN THE RACE. I RAN THE FOOTRACE. THAT WAS SET BEFORE ME ALL ACROSS THIS LAND. I DIDN'T HAVE ENOUGH WATER TO SUSTAIN THE MILES, DAYS AND NIGHTS TO BE A MESSENGER. How fast were the footsteps pressing down? / How wide the footprint, wide the stride?

ELEKTRA: Oh my god Orestes. For you the tears well up, for you the tears roll down.

ORESTES: ALL ALONG THE AQUEDUCTS. SCANT TREES, BRAZEN SCORPIONS OF SINEW, GRIM TEETHED FLAMING OF MY MUSCLES, STRIVE AND WRESTLE AS I MAY AGAINST THE FIXED POINT VANISHING. AND WHO WITH THE MIGHT OF SPEAR? AND WHO WITH HAND UPON THE HILT? KNOCK KNEES KNOCKING ONE MORE FOOT AND ONE MORE FOOTPRINT. I DISEMBODY JUST TO STAY IN MOTION. I REMEMBER WHAT I HAVE TO TELL YOU, I REHEARSE TO TELL YOU ALL ALONG THE AQUEDUCTS I KEEP REPEATING TO MYSELF TO TELL YOU JUST SO I CAN FALL DEAD AS THE MESSAGE LEAVES MY LIPS ...JUST REMEMBER YES OR NO. THUMBS UP, THUMBS DOWN. JUST REMEMBER ONE OF THESE THUMBS AND TELL YOU WHO / AND WHO IS DEAD

ELEKTRA & IPHIGENIA: And who. And who… *[refrain]*

ORESTES: WE STRIVE AND WRESTLE WITH THE FLESH. WE RUN THE RACE! WE NEVER SURRENDER! WE NEVER RETREAT! WE LIFT OUR WEAPONS! AND WE GRIP THE GRIP! WE GO FORTH ON THE EVIDENCE! TO THE VICTORY VISIBLE! WE SHUDDER TO THINK OF DEATHS COLD TERRORS, IN THE HARM OF SOME STRAY SNIPE OR BLOODBATH! WE BELIEVE THAT WE ARE PLURAL. WE BELIEVE IT IS IMPOSSIBLE TO LIVE A LIFE UNTARGETED. AND WE FLEX OUR MUSCLES. As did Orestes flex his muscless.

ELEKTRA & IPHIGENIA: And who with the might of spear. / And who with hand upon the hilt. And who… *[refrain]*

ORESTES: As did Orestes barrelling TOO CLOSE TO THE PILLAR in a tragic chariot disaster. As did Orestes lash his whips across the horses' flanks, their tendons straining and their muscles bulging, foaming at the mouth on the evidence to the victory visible. And then when fancy soars aloft, when shock on shock, the crash of chariots, the whole race strewn with the wreck of chariots, ripped asunder, horselegs torn from sockets and the axle box—as did Orestes! Rising from the gore, as did Orestes stagger to his knees, try to mount the horsemeat writhing, to win the race, he did NOT MISS-STEP ANY CRUCIAL HALF-STEP OF THE RIVETED UNISON, ill-fated for the clank of iron ringing through his brain. To dash the cup of bliss. He breathed to me his last I breathe to you: All my love to my family!

ELEKTRA and ORESTES embrace

ORESTES: Elektra, don't forget about your Daddy's hands. I am God's horseman and a Star without a Stain.

DEUS EX MACHINA: Children are memory's voices and preserve the dead from wholly dying. Ever buoyant in the depth submerged this wail of ours. Doth rise. Doth save.

costumes by Nancy Brous, set/lights by Allen Hahn (Here Atrs Ctr, NYC)

Act V. RED PILLARS

Scene 1: "Parlour"

Parlour room tension you could cut with a knife and 5/4 waltz timing. PEASANT HUSBAND replicates ORESTES' behavior as gentleman caller. AEGISTHUS gets a bass/abusive tone of voice commanding ELEKTRA to serve the wine; tenor/polite when speaking to ORESTES.

CLYTEMNESTRA: So did you hear the one about the fullbodied, smoky bouquet and very velvet, vintage... well the bottom of the glass had cracked a smile, smiling back at the boy until his head split open, / he was a dumb boy...

AEGISTHUS: Feedin time at the zoo.

CLYTEMNESTRA: Might as well drink straight rubies! We live like gods around here, pull up a chair!

AEGISTHUS: Well sure

ORESTES: Of course. *[he drinks]*

CLYTEMNESTRA: What do you think.

ORESETES: Very deep red.

AEGISTHUS *[aside to ELEKTRA]* Ggggget the stick girl, fetch the stick. Get in the house... *[to ORESTES]* Nothin but grim around here, To the lady, born to terrify!

CLYTEMNESTRA: We call it crimson.

ORESTES: That's pretty funny.

CHRYSOTHEMIS: I can never tell if she means a sacrifice or a joke.

AEGISTHUS: Show him the hearth honey, yeah I'll drink to you with all o'that fertility, god knows I look like a wad of gristle but I can fuckin bet on the horses. *[to Elektra]* Ggget in the house, ggget in there

CHRYSOTHEMIS: We can't find a prince to rend Elektra's prison walls.

AEGISTHUS: Ding dong! We get the prize! We get to wait for Elektra to get married! [God your neck, it's like it's inside out, it's like a lipstick sticking outta...]

CLYTEMNESTRA: You know I miss my baby. Poor little bright red bundle and her little lips slammed shut, I couldn't get a spoon in there...

AEGISTHUS: How 'bout we slay a bull. I think it's time to slay a bull, you get me. Talkin about blood ties, do ya get me.

ELEKTRA *[to herself, restrained]*: OH YEAH YOU BASK, YOU BASK, YOU TICKLE UP YOUR FANCY LIZARD SPEWING YOU

CHRYSOTHEMIS: Sorry excuse of a dead baby joke.

CLYTEMNESTRA: Let's not be crude. I hear those Thessalonians can slay a bull in one clean gash but we can get you a warm bath tonight, you tell your friends about our garden *[she spills a little wine]* Here's to the athlete! God knows we heave 'em to the lions. Tell your friends about this rivulet and broidered coils, Do they say anything about my baby? Iphigenia? It means sugar, Over there in, where'd you come from?

CHRYSOTHEMIS: Waitin for some lucky guy to smash that ugly, ugly, bug *[bursts of giggles]*

CLYTEMNESTRA: Oh honey look at that. Oh God. I've had a boo boo honey, help me. Help. *[her breasts begin to rupture]*

ELEKTRA: Orestes. I recognized you by your voice.

ORESTES: No kidding. And did they.

ELEKTRA: Those are the very red hands she slaughtered Daddy with.

CLYTEMNESTRA: Indeed! If you addressed me in such tone, I'd always hear you without pain.

CHRYSOTHEMIS: We always have to cut her down and bite her head off then we shackle her! Because Elektra's mean, she's mean to me you know so who cares!

CLYTEMN:	ELEKTRA:
SHE KNOWS NOTHING, ABSOLUTELY NOTHING ABOUT BABIES	I want her eyes to light on nothing. 'Til she knows the sword

CLYTEMNESTRA: Her father's blood was no relation to me and I watched him hover at my baby's throat like a wolf. *[lullabye agony]* With his red, red sword, My baby's blood red spray, Her lips in terror parted.

ORESTES: By the way do you ever get the feeling that you're at somebody's house for dinner and... And brushing by your knee ...you feel this... presence by your knee below your knee that's not like anything you know about these people and it's different and you're thinkin don't... look down there, don't act like you're... what the hell was that? Was that one of the kids? Startin to crawl? A dog of some sort? Sposed to be tied up out back? So you keep talking to the people, focus on whatever subject. Then it goes away and then it's cool. You're cool.

CHRYSOTHEMIS *[To ORESTES as if stripping to appease a rapist]:* Is she offending you? I'm not married either. I'm not usually like this. But I'm tired of the sacrifices.

CHRYSOTHEMIS [cont'd]: I wish we could pray to
the gods to keep us from the *quarter rest to lip to slit
voice*—keep us from slipping into every gash we
think could happen to us, flowing down the stones
where we were at each other's throats. It swallows
all the people and my voice was just a scarlet
thread-in-the-jericho about to be ruined by
trumpets but I watch my mother pray. Nobody
knows my mother like I do. There's a whole other
side of her and I guess you could say I'm on her
side.

CLYTEMNESTRA: She was a blurry wild creature,
Frolicking until he caught her by the neck…[*her
womb and breasts are hemorrhaging*]

ELEKTRA [*kissing ORESTES on his mouth, touching
his sword as he draws*]: Straight to the snare.

ORESTES: So the plan is this: we're gonna slash
the pillars red is why my sister called upon my
muscle and I think it's you and me.

***ORESTES marks AEGISTHUS' throat with a
slash.***

CLYTEMNESTRA: Oh my God he's got a sword.
Orestes and that girl have come to kill us.

Mercedes Bahleda as Cassandra (Here Arts Ctr, NYC)

56 ~ *The Elektra Fugues*

Act V, Scene 2:

"Lay Clean the Flank"

AEGISTHUS [bleeding]: Got a little riddle for you, yeah...So there's this uncle type a guy, step daddy creature, he steps in the family, shakin hands "How are ya people, oh ya look like sisters [to the mom] poor thing'is saggin to her knees, he butters that thing up, ya look like a movie, hell ya all look great, ya gotta real great place here, food's delicious, shot've whiskey for the lady, get down to the nieces

CLYTEMNESTRA: Aegisthus.

AEGISTHUS: "Whatcha learnin over there in school ya little sugar, plumb...daisy...dolly, is it terrible yet?" She pouts, "oh yes our uniforms are really scratchy"

CLYTEMNESTRA: They'll get the vault.

AEGISTHUS: And what comes after diapers, FOLKS, and two plus one is one plus two. No that's the uncle. Everybody! Pitch in! Help the lady out of wedlock, pin the diaper, diaper pin, what is that, don't stick the bottom with the pin, the clean diaper they said, please, hey you, [they'll always call on ya'monster] you gimme that diaper, wipe that off, let's put it this way...   in my business I seen buttocks in the air, I do what comes most natural and then I check outta those motels. Come noon, the girls start cleanin up the mess. Yeah I could wait around, check out the chambermaid, I'll maybe stay til one o'clock, don't wanta be exclusive.

CLYTEMNESTRA: They'll take everything.

AEGISTHUS: There's a whole other bedspread nobody even wrinkled! Baby doll, I'm bad with girls that pout, I'm bad with ages, bad with names, I'm not a bad guy so to speak but I'm half bad, that's enough.

CLYTEMNESTRA [*trying to contain her silicone pulp into her dress*]: I hate the Greeks, I hate the gods. I've seen em up close and they're nothing special.

AEGISTHUS: I'm a creature known as stepdaddy, "sugar daddy?" nope I'm broke but I can pay attention soon as you grow some little boobies... or maybe even sooner, Oh you get offended, FOLKS, if you don't get my jokes go ask the big guy, close your eyes and pray for me, he's the Guy that set up all my gigs, you stay with the real Daddy, none of this would happen and you know it. I'm just steppin in, don't glare at me, just gettin your moma happy, make her feel like high school. Too bad its the law of nature that you look a little more like first love, too bad I been framed but that's the way it is. Bang bang, thank you dolly, wipe that up there honey, shut the diaper. Everybody's shocked to death but everybody glared at me from day one, why is that? ARE YOU surprised why is that. Guilty by half-step, canNOT relate to buttocks in the family, in the air, in the magazine, beast of burden and I fit the bill. Truth of the matter is you need a whippin boy and I look like a shadow on the wall when you go back through the house so you can hate my guts.

ELEKTRA: Kill Aegisthus. He's the bonus.

ORESTES: God. I thought they were inpenetrable.

58 ~ The Elektra Fugues

ORESTES slits AEGISTHUS' throat.

AEGISTHUS: Get whatcha pay for and sooner or later we all.... get..... dirty..... Doncha. *[wink]* God you're gorgeous, Anybody here from New York City, thank you, thank you very much.

AEGISTHUS dies.

ELEKTRA: Devil took'im down like a B-flat but
God gave us the blues.

ORESTES: Oh God she bared her breast to me.

ELEKTRA: That's just a surface wound.

ORESTES: It's bleeding.

ELEKTRA: It just broke the skin—

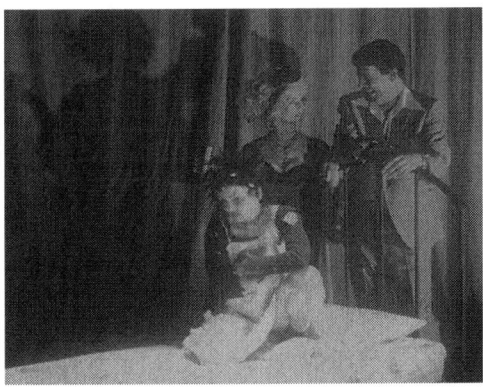

*Jennifer Griffin as Clytemnestra and Matthew Posey as Aegisthus
(Bottom's Dream Theater, LA)*

Act V, Scene 3:

"Cost of Driving"

CLYTEMNESTRA: Girl, do you know the cost of driving? All the way home from here? It gets expensive....To get down'ere....And sit down'ere at the table...As an astronaut. Did-you-think-it-would-be the SAME PLATE? Set to overflowing with thanksgiving? Go fetch the stick, girl, From the bright red prairie little house. And see if you can get it back together. With the fam'ly tree.....Get along home red-handed girl and you call it drivin drivin drivin. And you call it flyin flyin flyin. And you call it wolf ...wolf...wolf..... wolf.....

CLYTEMNESTRA implodes.

Act V, Scene 4:

"Flotsam Oracle"

CHRYSOTHEMIS: ....Approach on....a correction...we'll be standing by for you...and you can plan....and you can..... I'm sorry. This is not.... in any way...and you can plan....and you can...

ORESTES: Oh my god, Elektra. The patriarchy is a matriarchy!

ELEKTRA: Same old counter-revolution.

Act V, Scene 5: "Blood Songs"

Opening of choral tracks in black box recording of AGAMEMNON's crash site. Furies descend on ORESTES.

Lay clean the flank		Oh God a blow	Fair weather for the sky is red
Lay clean the red flank	One clean gash	Nothing but the red handed perishing Of you	
	And one red hour	A bright red blow	
Lay clean the flank	blood red spray	A mortal blow	Fair weather for the sky
Lay clean the red flank	and one clean gash	Another blow	Red sky at morning
Nothing but the blood of	Nothing but the blood of	And then another blow	Though your Sins	wine cup of my fury
Nothing but the blood of…	Nothing but the blood of…	Nothing but the blood of	Your sins be as scarlet	Nothing but the blood of
		Nothing but the blood of…	Nothing but the blood of	Nothing but the blood of
			Nothing but the blood of…	

62 ~ *The Elektra Fugues*

Act VI. GIRL-LIKE FACE

Scene 1: "Deus Ex Machina"

ELEKTRA comes upon the PEASANT HUSBAND after a very long time. He is eating a suspended spoonful of CHRYSOTHEMIS' food. ELEKTRA speaks to him as he whets his appetite as if between CHRYSOTHEMIS' thighs as she slowly bends to remove her apron in a long intake of breath, trying to mask her pleasure.

PEASANT HUSBAND: Don't you remember when I said I'd carry your books from school playing make believe you're married to me

ELEKTRA: You know your lips were the only thing I could ever read

PEASANT HUSBAND: Now I carry all these things in my heavy head, quite burdensome *[wink]*. But I showed up for the preface and that's something these days

ELEKTRA: *[wink]* Ask the god of the machine

PEASANT HUSBAND: I disagree with your ulterior negation, all this ending of the world, you see it is a lovely day, it's a bright day, all the streets are bright and we've got time to kill for a stroll for Sunday, drink a soda in the park and you can daydream and I'll pay. But then you'll go getting sharp. I realize that's your lack. Somebody somewhere has turned up your volume, blasted the speakers and now the little knob broke off. Abbreviating your poor fate.

ELEKTRA: Yeah I guess it must be hard to maintain an erection in the noise, face down in some similar orifice, what is that a gash? of quarter rest—to lip—to slit voice, maybe it feels good, do that, a little reverb on your static or my static [anybody else], yeah you hear the one about the choice between a garbage disposal and some lovin you know what they say I would choose

PEASANT HUSBAND: We don't need the modern riddles any more, I'm feeling your terrain of tiny obstacles, I'm feeling quite disgusted by the butchery.

ELEKTRA: Out of the blue, oh yes, you would have noticed my rotten teeth and wrinkles in the sunshine when we got down to the water, underneath the girdle. Isn't she the spittin image of my underage school pictures, when the waterfall was photocopied.

PEASANT HUSBAND: Now what's the trouble.

ELEKTRA: Was I frowning?

PEASANT HUSBAND: Now what's wrong

ELEKTRA: I didn't do anything

PEASANT HUSBAND: Now what is it

They start lying.

ELEKTRA: Too bad you won't be listed when the credits roll and I'll forget who you were playing

PEASANT HUSBAND: You know I travel frequently in my line of business

ELEKTRA: I'm sorry about the age difference

ELEKTRA presses PEASANT HUSBAND's spoon into a new wound in CHRYSOTHEMIS' throat, unable to resist the temptation. It bleeds again; CHRYSOTHEMIS makes gentle sounds as she dies.

Tim Maner as Peasant Husband and Director (Here Arts Ctr)

Act VI, Scene 2: "Slit Voice"

CHRYSOTHEMIS/IPHIGENIA: Does he? Notice my virginity? What do I —Look like closeup to the point where his eyes would cross? If I am a good enough liar, I can manufacture this repetition daily until we grow old. Does he? Notice I am already dead? Or does he think I've gotten makeup tricks from an excellent magazine? His military picture looks exactly like my Daddy…I get the idea he can afford the kind of furniture I need to simulate my existence…

PEASANT HUSBAND: I do

ORESTES [*running far away into the distance*] I do too

CHRYSOTHEMIS *climaxes as she dies.*

Act VI, Scene 3: "Black Box Recording"

ELEKTRA makes a final recording for ORESTES as she hovers in auto-pilot above the crash site of HER FATHER, watching the Furies tear after ORESTES eternally through the wilderness below.

ELEKTRA: ...So there'd be all this technical...velocity...for the air traffic control and then you'd hear me say I'm gonna go through one more puffy little cloud "good day to die" some sort've joke about my deathwish gonna take us down and you'd say "Oh God really? Do you even know how to fly?" which'd give me away as being scared to death of being airborne up here so divine, I know you wrecked your motorcycle. And then— blank...for whatever I could say. So I just say "not to expect" because "they told me not to expect to go up in his plane." So I quoted that and all the things I think about crashing... And they won't get any more information than that when we do go down. There'll be the pilots screaming...technical failure, stuff they'll go digging through the carnage for, and open it. I found out later they don't put black box recorders on those single engine planes because they're too small. And at the time nobody that knew me even knew I was up in the air.

PEASANT HUSBAND embraces CHRYSOTHEMIS as she emits a beautifully perfect pitch. Sound of a new recording. Pitch continues softly and eternally. Erasure.

early black box recorder

~ END OF THE ELEKTRA FUGUES ~

Nina Hellman as Penny, photo by Bob Handelman

RED FROGS:

a burlesque mirror for the summer purgatorio

by

Ruth Margraff

Introduction to RED FROGS

By Elyse Singer

The first time I heard RED FROGS was on Hourglass Group's summer retreat in Connecticut. It was our practice to read scripts aloud – *cold*—without prior rehearsal. Hearing the voices of Beatifica, the 'Og, Penny and the Coney Island girls, and experiencing the three-dimensional musicality and shimmering quality of the language, is really the optimal way to experience the language and world of this play. On the page, there is poetry, but experienced live—it is spectacle.

We developed RED FROGS over several readings and workshops between 2000 and 2002 in New York City and in Providence, RI. In the middle of this process, the world changed. After 9/11, Beatifica's thought balloons and the glass separating the real from the surreal, high art from low art, rich from poor, seemed even more slippery and Mabie's political agitation took on new meaning. The concepts of spectacle, beauty and human connection felt different too.

RED FROGS is really a dramaturg's playground, referencing Aristophanes' THE FROGS as well as historic Coney Island and contemporary talk shows. Not to mention Marx, Dolly Parton and Iraqi liberation movements. As part of our research for the premiere production at P.S. 122, we took the cast and design team to Coney Island to visit the Aquarium and Coney Island Museum. We rode the carousel and caught the rings. In design meetings, we came up with the concept of setting the play itself in an aquarium. The production was bursting with color, movement and surreally comic touches. The set had a gigantic red crab hanging on the edge, while the opposite wall had a giant tip of a yellow mustard bottle protruding out, which doubled as the 'Og's airplane. The 'Og's coat was a fur coat made from "dead" stuffed animals sewn together. Projections of water merged into wave-like patterns created by sequined fabric, and we incorporated images from early 20th Century Coney Island as well.

RED FROGS is one of Ruth's only plays written without music and not conceived as a new opera. In some ways, the script is a protest against conventional dramatic form: the spoken language in RED FROGS presses up against the "glass ceiling" of stage realism just as the Coney Island working girls shimmy and burlesque themselves against the glass walls of the Aquarium. Words resonate as they slip by or slip away, like the missing capital of the Shaggy 'Og and the rooftop of Pilar's dog house.

The script for RED FROGS is as close as you can get to opera without actual singing. It's meant to be experienced live and to inspire wonder...just like Coney Island. But, at the same time, when you experience it live, the humanity shines through the spectacle and the characters become very real indeed.

So hang on tight to the safety rail, and enjoy the ride!

Elyse Singer has had the great pleasure of collaborating with Ruth Margraff since 1994 on her plays *Flags Unfurled: 1976, Wallpaper Psalm, Red Frogs* and, more recently, *Wellspring*. As Founding Artistic Director of Hourglass Group, she directed and produced the world premiere of the first US revivals of Mae West's plays *SEX* and *Pleasure Man* (with Charles Busch); the OBIE-Award winning *Trouble in Paradise*; Deborah Swisher's *Hundreds of Sisters & One BIG Brother*; and her original multi-media play *Frequency Hopping* at 3LD (winner, 2007 International STAGE Script Competition). Other original works include *Love in the Void; Private Property* and *Care-less: Eva Tanguay*. As Off-Broadway producer: *Beebo Brinker Chronicles* (GLAAD Media Award). She is a Usual Suspect at NYTW, an alum of the Lincoln Center Theater Directors Lab and a member of LPTW and SDC.

*character sketch "hung by serving trays divine comedy" with feather duster feathers by
Ruth Margraff (courtesy of Gretchen van Lente)*

Acknowledgments

RED FROGS was first published in *American Theatre* magazine Vol. 19 No. 9 by Theatre Communications Group November, 2002. RED FROGS premiered at P.S.122 [Mark Russell, Executive Director] February 28—March 24, 2002 co-produced by Hourglass Group

Director: Elyse Singer

set design: Juman Malouf; lighting design: Traci Klainer; costume design: Kaye Voyce; sound design: Laura Grace Brown; projection design: Elaine J. McCarthy; Dramaturgy: Erika Rundle.

Molly Powell .... Beatifica Strata

Nina Hellman....................Penny Shaw

Steven Rattazzi.................The Shaggy 'Og

Crystal Bock.....................Dolly Dallas

Nicole Lowrance..................Shirley Goodness

Stacey Karen Robinson................Mabie Main

RED FROGS was commissioned by P.S.122 with funds provided by the Jerome Foundation, made possible in part by the Fund for Creative Communities/New York State Council on the Arts Decentralization Program, administered by the Lower Manhattan Cultural Council. RED FROGS received development through workshops at Bottom's Dream Theater/A.S.K. Theater Projects [Ian Belton, director; Jim Martin, director], New York Theatre Workshop, Hourglass Group and The Perishable Theatre [Elyse Singer, director]. It was also read in English at the Bolshoi Zal for Rachel Perimeter's Moskva Contemporary American Series in July 2002, with the support of the Library for Foreign Literature and Arts International [Moscow, Russia].

Roles:

NANTUCKET ISLAND SUMMER FOLK:

BEATIFICA STRATA, herself—*[A superwoman in the Shaw sense. Speaks clearly as if voiced-over from a bird's-eye. Has ascended to Upper Bourgeois Realism as a talking-headed-pundit, but during the typhoon revolution of the play, slips into a side project of writing a historical-romance-novel exploiting her maid's distress. Tries to convince the over-the-counter roofless sufferers that deep down it is really all one Essentially Geocentric Paradise to, for instance, have a younger husband and a summer home, and assets that she earned with her Ivy-League education. And she knows exactly how they feel, until she loses her temper and has them flogged.*

THE SHAGGY 'OG, descendant of Karl Marx and kept husband of Beatifica Strata—*[Bitter propagandist who had preached the decadent waste of Coney Island as a parody of Socialism with no use value other than imitation. Washed up on Nantucket when he dropped out of the Ivy League to be a summertime landscaper and found himself a kept husband. When he realizes Beatifica's superpower in the world, his intellect renders him parasitic to her wealth, an intimate position from which he hopes to bring the system down around its ears. Has a suspicious tail that women try to perpetually castrate.]*

PENNY SHAW, Beatifica's maid—*[A recently disrupted Dostoyevskian Baptist from San Antonio, who has somehow gotten through one or two chapters of the Marx & Engels reader, but still has bills to pay. Her mother had gotten an earlier start at Mabie Main's boarding house but then went belly up down South. Her mother worked for BEATIFICA and Beatifica's mother, cleaning their homes and the Calico Cupboard in downtown Nantucket, but never had the capital to really back up the leap in class. A turquoise-eyed girl working her way through college, with chronic nightmares of herself topstitched to the throat in a cowboy boot after being dragged from the back of a still confederate pick-up truck.]*

Roles [cont'd]:

CONEY ISLAND GIRLS:

MABIE MAIN—*[A proletariat native of Nantucket who ran a boarding house for Ivy League girls, after her fisherman lover ran off to his liquor. Mabie fled the island after her daughter killed herself with a Marxist utopia too grand for her mother's waterbed. She fled to Coney Island and said she'd never go back to that cursed Gray Lady place. Mabie has been making a living by reading palms in the forehead of the Trojan Frog casino as a tribute to the publicly executed Elephant Frog of early Coney lore. She once rivaled Dolly for a fisherman that talked her ear off on her police radio.]*

DOLLY DALLAS—*[Born in Dallas, ran off to West Virginia with a coal miner and a daughter out of wedlock. Double frosted hair, hubcap knees and bedroom one-liners tossed over her significant bosom, Dolly has been burlesquing in Coney Island in the replicated Fall of Pompeii, Dragon's Gorge and the Switchback Railroad for some time. Sometimes works as a soda jerk girl, where she tries to stay in shape by go-go dancing in pool stick powder blue tassels and quarters for the juke box. Obsessed with fantasies of coal mining on the roller coasters. Has no health insurance, so takes fistfuls of Migraine aspirin over-the-counter].*

SHIRLEY GOODNESS—*[Runaway daughter of Dolly Dallas. Ran into her mother in Little Egypt, Coney Island, when she was swallowing a sword. Dolly takes Shirley back under her wing in the Coney Island Rescue Mission for Wayward Girls. They live a fatherless life on the lamb out of cars, with Dolly home-schooling Shirley in the entertainments, with nowhere to really plug in a television set. Used to sing and baby burlesque when she was a small and curly charmer. Very good with making hair much bigger and blonder than it was and is the bastard of a coal miner she knows nothing about.]*

Time

Turn of the Purgatorial Century.

Place

A glass box theatre, with aquarium backdrops of amusement...An imagineered purgatorio, between the seascapes of Coney Island and Nantucket Island, where Beatifica's glass house overlooks a stretch of expensive, waterfront real estate. At times there seem to be *glass ceilings* or a *glass-bottomed boat* restraining the confidence of efforts to overtake Beatifica's opulent place in the American economy for reality-based entertainment. For the Coney Island Girls, Penny and the 'Og: to get one's foot in the door is to save oneself from working-class Hell on earth and to go instead to bourgeois Heaven.

Author's Notes

All stage directions are written to inspire performance and not to be taken literally. This play delightfully burlesques most conventions of realism for the more imaginary possibilities of surreality. Anything that seems pretentious in the language should be performed with bad teeth on the verge of mispronunciation and irreverence but with conviction. RED FROGS was inspired by Aristophanes' FROGS, the idea of a truly female Charlie Chaplin and a divine comedy burlesqued as a Marxist "ruthless critique of everything existing" and by the Iraq Liberation Action Committee [merged with the Iraq National Congress of Washington and London], for which the playwright hosted a symposium on July 10, 2001, at HERE Arts Center. This gathering attracted diplomats, former CIA agents and an Iraqi Opposition guerilla warrior Al-Battat, who was tortured a week later by Turkish officials who threatened to execute him in Baghdad when he deplaned, none of which ever reached the American press.

For the tycoon mother and daughter I cleaned for in Nantucket, as did my mother the summer before. For Elyse, Thalia Field, Fred Ho and Omar (a pseudonym of course).

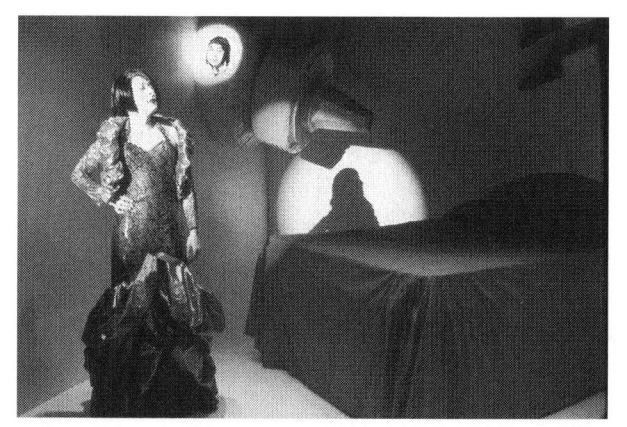

Molly Powell as Beatifica (PS122, NYC)

RED FROGS:

a burlesque mirror for the summer purgatorio

by

Ruth Margraff

Coin #1: Sea Level Upheave

BEATIFICA STRATA unleashes a media typhoon with one of her thought balloons, washing some sunburned over-the-counter girls from Coney Island toward Nantucket Island. BEATIFICA surveys it from her Nantucket picture window while the SHAGGY 'OG hovers with her opera glasses and glass-bottomed single-engine plane.

Forward slashes [/] indicate overlapping dialogue.

BEATIFICA STRATA: I want my opera glasses back. Don't break them. Don't use my things, Karl. Put my airplane back. I can see you from my picture window!

SHAGGY 'OG: But I'm hovering. You told me to hover for you.

BEATIFICA: Not in my single-engine, glass-bottomed plane. Go up with the traffic people or something. I don't want my plane in the public eye / I have a migraine.

SHAGGY 'OG: Your plane *is* the public eye, my dear tycoon.

BEATIFICA: Don't call me a tycoon, Karl, get down.

SHAGGY 'OG: Caller #3 not on the air. Standby.

BEATIFICA: Karl, no, don't take their calls. Get rid of them.

SHAGGY 'OG: Never never, baby, standby.

BEATIFICA: They stalk me then they hate me. Talk talk talk. I hate their stupid drivel. Every day. I hate my studio audience.

SHAGGY 'OG: Oh great that just got broadcast! A typhoon! Triggered by one of your thought balloons! Upheaving an ultraviolet Hellgate ride in Coney Island! I can't shut it off

BEATIFICA: They wanna climb on me, don't they Karl? Take over the show, run up their own wave of hype or something. Pulp and gristle?

CONEY ISLAND GIRLS: Pulp and gristle...Pulp and gristle...

BEATIFICA: I'm sick of feigning interest in their conventional wisdom. Sick of needing my opera glasses everywhere I go to keep me head-and shoulders above all that overweight, underpaid drudgery that drags them down into the cotton candy spit of my studio audience *[Bleep]*.

CONEY ISLAND GIRLS: Cotton candy spit typhoons you mean from Coney Island?! Hellooooo Nantucket superlady!

BEATIFICA: I could publish one of my thoughts in a historical romance novel thinly veiled as my memoir! If I had someone I could talk to on my level. I talk down all day. It's maddening. *[aside]* Even Karl is beneath me.

SHAGGY 'OG [*Viewing her through opera glasses*]: There is a typhoon situation heading right your way – can you not hear me, Beatifica?

BEATIFICA: I do my best to keep my talking head still talking.

CONEY ISLAND GIRLS: Coney Island to Nantucket Island whoohooo!!!

BEATIFICA: Coney Island is the fop of our entire century! A hellish place where even the Fall of Pompeii gets imagineered as a sort of bacchanal roller coaster. Don't make me talk to Coney Island, Karl!

SHAGGY 'OG: I am a menace to myself. A lover of the art that shall refine me. Rather than the art that causes me to suffer. Nor the art that shall uplift the others, sadly, no. "Coney dogs" we'll brand this storm of sunburned gristle shoved back on a stick. The great ungirdling of amusement! Ah the wigs and hips alurch in the teeth of what? A ferris wheel?

Coney Island Girls burlesque for the public eye:

DOLLY DALLAS: Heya TV I'm Dolly Dallas! Homeschoolin' my pipsqueak outta my car to save up for my GED.

SHIRLEY GOODNESS: I'm Shirley Curly Goodness! Worryin' about the lie detector test and peein' in a Pixie cup.

MABIE MAIN: Mabie Main here—buck up or I'll wrap your presents at the Mall.

SHIRLEY: I can maybe talk about my mama's feather dusting two fer one on the daytime soapset of your life, you wanna peak-a-boo? Com' on. *[Kiss, kiss]*

DOLLY: That's my baby gulpin' aspirin for thuh over-the-counter workers comp haha!

SHIRLEY: Mama sure uplift the furniture, dear Lord, to get at the dust bunnies!

MABIE: Once got a grand piano right between the eyes.

CONEY ISLAND GIRLS: Tippin' off my servin' tray!

DOLLY: We hum a little ballet scrubbin' on all fours.

MABIE: Whip't to the side, mind you, to ward off the harassin' with a grain uh salt!

CONEY ISLAND GIRLS: Bent over backwards like our mamas, ow oh! Clown for Sure!

MABIE: Hey ain't you whatchalla upscale shaggy lapdog that lost his, um, initial capital? *[Wink]*

SHAGGY 'OG: So you people…Coin your first I believe it's "ruthless critique of everything existing" which you probably misread in the 4th edition.

BEATIFICA: You should go back to college Karl. Get some of your anger down on paper.

SHAGGY 'OG: We will live through this disaster. It will feel real.

Drops down to deliver opera glasses to BEATIFICA before he runs whimpering into her bedroom. The Coney Island Girls flail against the picture window like they are in a typhoon.

BEATIFICA: Ugh! To think they used to press their suctions up against my glass-bottomed boat. And we'd have the offspring point, "And that one's belly up," and "That's what we call pink eye." See the sea lions roaring in their bubbles! Look at the tusk scuffs that the angry walrus makes!

MABIE: We dunno the grand Atlantic is across the boardwalk. [*Wink*]

DOLLY & SHIRLEY: We ain't two-headed babies, lady.

MABIE: We just work a little harder, that's all.

BEATIFICA [*Recovering her talk show persona*]: It's me! Voicing over all your tufts of hope inside your shrunken thought balloons! Where you have hoarded nothing but profanity. Even I, you see, once lay down with a downtown boy who was disheveled in so many ways. No ready-made critique of himself. Barely dressed. And he pressed down on my mouth like it was some sort of file left open for the double-clicking of his mouse!

SHIRLEY: And that's your most traumatic moment?

BEATIFICA: I swam one summer in the public reservoir, oh yes. And I recycle all my cans. I think of you Coney creatures and your human rights. I use mass transit when I'm in New York. I blow big kisses to the deli boys hopping down beneath my sandwich. But I'm safe now so good night. Quick, Penny, turn on the security or I'll have you flogged.

SHIRLEY: There is a lot of trouble in the world.

MABIE: And Beatifica Strata to dub the voiceover of reason onto it, thank you!!

BEATIFICA: Penny! Get my list of questions I will answer...Penny! As opposed to Dog'n Sudsiness. And the real Nantucket Ocean will be downloaded back to sea level where it belongs

MABIE: Like we can't adjust to the assembly required on a rogue missile.

SHIRLEY & DOLLY: God save the parasitic possibility.

BEATIFICA: So what. Self-help yourselves!

MABIE: Talk.

CONEY ISLAND GIRLS: Talk talk.

BEATIFICA bravely ducks outside for a soundbyte holding up her opera glasses in the typhoon.

BEATIFICA: I've...got a maid. I...treat my husband like a dog. End of my story. Penny! Are you here? I will never...throw in the towel of American Upper Realism as a, er, dogmatic abstraction. Cheerio!

MABIE: There goes my roof! And my daughter's doghouse roof! Is floating by my hair! Pilar!

SHIRLEY *[Aside]:* She went to the doghouse to think things over? Poor thing. Who is Pilar?

BEATIFICA *runs inside and slams the door.*

BEATIFICA: Nothing swept up, 'Og-fur everywhere! *[Enters, exits]* Penny! Penny! Nothing swept up! 'Og-fur everywhere! *[Enters, exits]*

PENNY SHAW *[In a bright red apron, mocks her]:* Nothing swept up! 'Og fur everyhere!

BEATIFICA: You lolly-gagger, ooh, I'll beat you silly!

SHIRLEY: Under the picture window, quick, and grab some chapstick!

BEATIFICA: Penny! Penny! Turn on the security!

PENNY: I can't. It's run amok.

BEATIFICA: I don't want to be seen. Ever again. Do you understand?

BEATIFICA *passes out cold.*

costumes: Kaye Voyce, projections: Elaine J. McCarthy (PS122 NYC)

Coin #2: Flogging

Inside BEATIFICA's summer home, all hierarchy has broken loose. Her maid PENNY has taken advantage of the Coney disaster to masquerade as BEATIFICA and rule over THE SHAGGY 'OG by flogging him. BEATIFICA answers the door or punishes PENNY amidst fainting spells as if she has lost all the reality-based reason that made her a tycoon. Meanwhile, the Coney Island Girls rival PENNY for her maid job, utilizing whatever labor skills they had before the upheaval.

PENNY *[disguised as BEATIFICA]*: Quit it...quit your yelpin', 'Og, or I will flog you silly. Gimee that, it's not a bone. *[To Coney Island Girls, imitating BEATIFICA's confession]* "I ain't home, oh um. I mean, I have a maid, I have uh Shaggy 'Og kept husband and I do hack off his 'Og fur. Hope you all been drownt to death. Good riddance."

PENNY hacks at the fur of THE 'OG who has collapsed in a stupor on the floor, he yelps in delirium and pulls on PENNY's sleeve with his teeth and growls.

SHAGGY 'OG: Thief. Stop thief.

PENNY beats THE 'OG. He bites at her feather duster, which she hides in her sleeve. A struggle.

CONEY ISLAND GIRLS: Knock knock.

BEATIFICA*[Moaning]:* No pulp! No more!

PENNY *[Hacking at THE 'OG's tail]*: I um, need a minute with my Shaggy 'Og right now and can't appear full frontal. Goddamn Penny maid loves nothin' more'n vacuumin' his...shag... Got his barkin' tangled up in all my thought balloons!

SHAGGY 'OG: God help the pulp that help itself!

PENNY: No one here is dustin' now. There is no workin' goin' on.

SHAGGY 'OG: Help! Help! She's just the maid. Half-educated. Slackt. BEATIFICA is swooned.

PENNY: As I said this morning on my teleprompter, did? Ah? Not?? This Penny maid peer down into her vacuum where she hacked his 'Og fur, workin-her-way-through-college, whereas as Beatifica Strata...I nibble at my just desserts. Cheerio!

THE 'OG bites PENNY's other hand. She sips a bit of something from a soup pan.

SHAGGY 'OG *[Aside]*: Hm. That's my 'Og food.

PENNY does a spit take from the spoon, 'Og bites her foot.

PENNY: Across the caype...My 'Og an' I get up there in my glass bottom single-engine playne and spin around an afternoon up to the Caype! And then the vinyerrd!

PENNY pushes the Coney Island Girls back through door...Doorbell.

BEATIFICA: Good morning, are you-

PENNY, sucked out by the vacuum of the open door, pushes to get back in.

PENNY: Yes I am. I'm Penny! I'm the maid.

Breathless, slams door.

BEATIFICA: Oh yes. I hardly recognize your mother's features in that sunburn. Your mother worked for me.

PENNY: I know! She told me! And I worked for your mother too, she was very...how shall I put it...

BEATIFICA: Did she tell you I prefer Ivy League college drop-out handymen? To play with as they work, it's great fun.

PENNY: I'm a tomboy anyway.

PENNY throws a soup pan on THE 'OG's head, causing his bark to echo.

SHAGGY 'OG *[Aside]:* The real Beatifica Strata will arouse to this mistake and send you straight to hell. This is a parrot maid. She's parroting her betters— you can see her feather duster up her sleeve.

SHIRLEY: I'm gonna get that ribbidabuoy-Penny maid job!

MABIE: You don't have a chance in hell to get a ribbidabuoy summertime maid job.

Doorbell.

BEATIFICA *[Staggers to the door]:* Good morning, are you—

SHIRLEY [*With red apron on, her foot in door*]: Yes I am. I'm Shirley Goodness.

BEATIFICA: Oh good, Penny, thanks. I hardly recognize you in that sunburn, red flag of a face. Come in.

SHIRLEY [*Climbing with great difficulty into doorway*]: I used to work for that dog with 'is shirt off in your picture window. Yeah I worked for him.

PENNY [*Worried*]: I cleaned for your mother I remind you ma'am.

SHIRLEY: There's so many millionaires it's like they're the people and we ain't the people here, hm. Oh well.

BEATIFICA: That's nice. You the people. Well I hope you can get over anything that's unprofessional.

SHIRLEY: Under your wing, no sweat!

She's in. Slams door.

PENNY: To think of all the shining that's been done in here already...That I've <u>had</u> done, and spicked and spanned 'til you can see what's gotten done and what has not.

DOLLY [*Knocking with renewed enthusiasm now that SHIRLEY got in*]: We're aroused a b-bit by your ribbidabuoy—self-esteem!

SHIRLEY [*Wrinkles nose*]: Oh that.

PENNY [Aside]: That's nothing.

SHIRLEY [Aside]: That's a summertime n-gnat.

MABIE [Aside]: It's n-not.

DOLLY [Aside]: It's not?

PENNY [Covering her ears; pushing SHIRLEY out]: It's <u>my</u> job! Me I'm Penny!

SHIRLEY [Aside]: Was that commercially symbolic?

DOLLY: I don't know, let's check the old dollars.

They look at the back of some old dollars in their pockets. Have no idea how to interpret them and are terrified.

SHIRLEY: Hm.

THE 'OG puts up his talking head to picture window, flexing incredible muscles

SHAGGY 'OG: Oh say the vacuum gets to me

It sucks down all my energy

But I get better food than the housemaid does at college / Working her way through college

I lose a few tufts...in the pennies

At the corners of this summer home

But I would rather sleep all day

My castle is my mind when I'm alone...

Steven Rattazzi as The 'Og (PS122)

THE 'OG is beaten until a bald spot appears on his head and then tossed out a door with a kick to the ass. The Coney Island Girls gasp.

BEATIFICA: I'm sorry but I've gone the other way. Down down. My part-time yellow journalism has—

BEATIFICA & PENNY: Receded—

BEATIFICA: Into a very grand but trashy historical romance novel I'll be writing in my rustic attic. And only my maid—

SHAGGY 'OG: And 'Og—

BEATIFICA: And 'Og will know what I really do.

DOLLY [*Pushing her head in door*]: In the voice of reason, I! Can safely say you should be writin' down the talkin' of the heretofore housemaid....cocksure and the cuckold Mr. Beatifica probly give her 'is rib. It is then that she'll stop imitatin' you and find her future cumulus so-called hairspray. [*Door slammed on her head*] Ow!

The door keeps slamming on DOLLY's head.

SHAGGY 'OG: An' laid her leg bare for the humping!

'Og begins to hump legs slammed in door.

MABIE [*Aside*]: We hear it's old money—

DOLLY [*Aside*]: From her Calico mama—

SHAGGY 'OG: They never toss me a bone. That's Why I'm neck-ed in this summertime fog. Confusing my winter coat that tries to grow in a tickless clock.

Doorbell.

BEATIFICA: Oh g'lord. Good morning, are you—

MABIE: Yes I am.

BEATIFICA: Oh yes. I hardly recognize your—daughter's work...loaded down with rivets in the cheeks, and do you dance and sing?

MABIE: Yes, ma'am. They tell me Domesticity [*Small laugh*] has little variation but improvement.

BEATIFICA: That sounds familiar, yes.

MABIE: Just one foot in the door is all.

BEATIFICA: From the superneck up since I stepped on many necks to get to where I am!

MABIE: They'd all be paperback who cares.

SHIRLEY: Your mama just has cobwebs so I wouldn't know!

PENNY is choked by SHIRLEY GOODNESS who steps forward.

BEATIFICA: Red flag with the sunburn, missy?

SHIRLEY [*Brightly*]: It's a sort of birthmark. My mother was roasted half to death in a life-size danse du ventre Double Eros. I run into her red handed—she was swallowin' a sword.

BEATIFICA: They have a Little Egypt in Coney Island now? Really?

MABIE: Really.

SHIRLEY *[Schmoozing]*: Oh when we was green...the wildcats'd get my mama twirling in her underwear in circles up the mountains. She blew the coal an' buried mushroom clouds with one old shovel to the belly of it. *[Softshoe tap dance]* Got herself black lung 'n' granny spit tobacco...Betcha thought it looked like turquoise in there or the Seaside two days off? My mama told me Shirley, betcha you could be a charmer of a babysweet burlesque, you got the curly headed awe to charm that is. *[She yawns]*

BEATIFICA: At least you've got ambitions toward reality. That is a sort of gift. Now then.

MABIE MAIN grabs PENNY by the hair, drags her out into the upheaval.

DOLLY: Get 'er by the face and pull!

MABIE: That face is scuffed and dull from circulation!

PENNY: I'll take the 'Oghouse, 'Og. Oh please, and no bowl, I don't give a damn about a roof. But not to Hell please—

CONEY ISLAND GIRLS *[From doors ajar]*: Talk.

PENNY: I am.

CONEY ISLAND GIRLS: Talk with your head.

PENNY: I try.

CONEY ISLAND GIRLS: Keep talking.

MABIE: In a bell tone, please.

PENNY: Uh...Uh...

MABIE: Her head shrinks when she talks. As if she'd kiss a Marxist in the shadow of his brim to get minutiae. *[Kisses PENNY on the mouth]*

SHIRLEY: Ultraviolet to efface her!

PENNY: Here I go to Hell—

BEATIFICA *[Phone rings; Coney Island Girls hide]*: Cheerio, was she assertive with you, Karl? Uh-huh. Grown cheeky overnight. Is that so? Well I've got my own darts killing me. So, flog her, okay, yes, distinctly...cheerio. *[Swoons]*

PENNY *[Contrite, rings doorbell]*: I...uhm...promise to restore the dusted knick-knacks to their shelves. And get down on my fours. And jump when you say jump. But...more and more red grows every day. And more blush that I uh...I swear you're planting in my purse from your purse which I try to sort of pull up by the bootstraps.

SHIRLEY *[Aside to 'OG]*: Beat her 'til she weeps.

DOLLY: Beat her 'til she's hygiened.

BEATIFICA *[Sleepwalking to the door]*: Just while you're cleaning, Penny, please. This is not a live-in situation. *[Answers doorbell, finds PENNY on her knees]* Why, hello there. It's so lovely, all these real misfortunes I've been pressing into one long paperback... historic *[Hiccup]* romance...of when we were green...jumping at the chance. Even Karl had his tree frogs all in a bell jar...we would swat at the tether ball all summer long with hands like gloves and glide across the placid mirror back when the typhoon was a ripple and I would lean...upside down from my water bike and let my tongue touch on the glass of the Lake of…

BEATIFICA *[cont'd. Burns her tongue on doorway, steps back]*... Wildfire. What kind of flogging do you want to have? To cover up your bloody pulp?

BEATIFICA assigns a beating of PENNY. The Coney Island Girls carry it out. BEATIFICA swoons again.

PENNY: I'm used to it.

PENNY & SHIRLEY: Kickin' like a cowboy boot.

PENNY: I'd like to stay the same.

MABIE: The same?

As she is slapsticked, losing her apron:

PENNY: When I was green. It was summer all the time in the Deep South and every household was a summer home. We frolicked in the lily pads as the professional water bikes went by. I told my mama I could grow large as you. Much more colossal than you'd think I'd grow up to. Out of tadpoles of a naked eye. Which children will get overthrown with half an education? What were we learnin' in the chalk...as you leaned so slightly forward into the darts of your blouse? What if we adjust to wildfire as if it wuz an iron skillet? Bent down like a willow on some china plate in your mama's hutch. What will you go back into the fire for, Ms. Strata? I erect myself upon my stake, disrobing at your wariness. *[Disrobes herself of BEATIFICA's summer outfit, Coney Island Girls hide. Ties her apron back on in front of BEATIFICA's scrutiny]* I dream of all your feathers in my cap. I'd stalk you in faint films of light and kiss your cousins. But never fear. I'm swelling from my dropsy to the bulbous shape of a lute!

PENNY dives into the skirts of BEATIFICA, head first with feather duster.

100 ~ *Red Frogs*

Nina Hellman as Penny (PS122)

SHAGGY'OG: It's her misfortune, not her fault, that she's un-neck-ed.

BEATIFICA: I recommend the guillotine if we can pull out something from that socket of an intellect. To hack at. Oh, I am coming to my senses, what? Oh here I am...I'm here. Was there an afternoon where we locked gazes or is there nothing in the poor's heads but vengeance as they say? My maid is burrowing for—Oh...I feel a small...appreciation. I feel small...slippings...of the lip...like some sort of clown is slipping in his wallpaper paste!

She shudders with pleasure.

PENNY: My mouth's still watering, madam. I desire...to but dip...the burning tip of the flick...of my tongue...

PENNY goes back down on BEATIFICA.

BEATIFICA: I'll...oh...yes, quit the romancing of my history over yours, if we discover...what were thought to be rose-colored bones. I'll remove your tint of struggle—oil painted in your loss. And beat the part of you that's sticking out! Fasten and then pull! If there be such a stem in this horrifying pulp!! *[Laughs and trembles; aside]* We will be sick, all of us, now. We'll want it every afternoon. You'll beg me and if not, I'll beg you with a sidelong glance and then someday I will. Oh, oh. Reciprocate. *[Touches feather duster]* I'm sorry Poke...I was poking at it with my...hmm...and thought you'd twitch.

Coney Island Girls hop up out of hiding to dust and clean around BEATIFICA's aftermath; sharply:

102 ~ Red Frogs

BEATIFICA: How much help do I need, Penny?

BEATIFICA whirls on heel to see PENNY with the Coney Island Girls hidden behind her in a line, an optical illusion from BEATIFICA's point of view.

BEATIFICA: I don't care take the check and go. Don't break the sand dollar on the sink. Karl dove down to the ocean floor for that at least and got pink eye.

Red Frogs directed by Elyse Singer co-produced by Hourglass Group (PS122)

PENNY *[Starting to tremble with the innate impulse to leapfrog muffled behind her]*: I'll be careful. I'll be very quiet.

Coin #3: Begging Favor from a Corpse

The Coney Island Girls manage to get in the door but aren't able to maintain this positioning. As they are tossed out and toss out THE 'OG and PENNY, they get more envious of the summer home. They notice THE 'OG's Marxist rhetoric and try to hack off his tail-like concealed weapon, though it causes them to jump at chances and to conclusions like bones.

MABIE *[beginning to panic]*: I miss the pharmacy. I want to go back under the counter. To thuh crush've juggling and the Steeplechase. The squirting of the water pistols down the chute to the glass lagoon. I never could live up to the intellectual architecture of this place. And it. Streamlined my Pilar beneath its buttress. She couldn't keep her mind still, it kept jumpin' to conclusions, jumpin' at the chances tossed to her like the bones of a tycoon boy. Got her jittery and then she couldn't get her high brow up to pedastal she never growed between her shoulder blades...It tossed her up against the staircase grandeur college. Oh she got a tycoon husband on her little hook but she would cry up in my waterbed, oh Mommy, how'm I gonna wake up to that shirtless tycoon every day and sink back in my muck of flaws, my opalescent varicosity of thigh laid bare and humped at in his eye. I'd say you tiptoe down to your appliances—muster up thuh corpor-ately drippin', blinkin' office of a superwife and lie right through your bad teeth. But we was both too sad to keep our cuffs rolled up and down the shore in some forever promenade of...uh...how shall I put it...

THE 'OG has been thumping his tail against MABIE's leg the whole time.

DOLLY: Get offa her.

MABIE: I don't mind.

DOLLY: There it goes again—what is that stump?

SHIRLEY: Stub I think, in there and bony like a snail spine in it!

MABIE: Gristle

DOLLY: Like a nostril?

MABIE: If a nostril wagged and didn't flare itself!

SHIRLEY: I'll take care of it, look out! *[Hacks at tail]*

DOLLY: I'll get it from the side! *[Hack, hack]*

SHAGGY 'OG *[Shielding crotch]*:

  No muscles, ma'am.

  It's fur and bone.

  I work it like a smile.

CONEY ISLAND GIRLS: Effortless?

SHAGGY'OG: Exactly.

SHIRLEY: I don't mind.

Tail becomes erect with her.

MABIE: If not, we can subtract it—

DOLLY & SHIRLEY: Right.

They hack off 'OG's arm.

SHIRLEY: Or see what else could wag with it subtracted.

They hack off 'OG's other arm.

PENNY: What's the use? *[She smiles]*

DOLLY: You want to marry one of us?

PENNY: You're penniless yourselves.

MABIE: So why'd you smile at us?

PENNY: More at you.

MABIE distracts PENNY with her Chaplin softshoe as she casually hacks off 'OG's opera glasses once and for all.

MABIE: Because of my concealed propensity for mustachioed swash-buckling?

PENNY: Yes and your...er...ah *[Whispers]*...place where your concealed weapon would be concealed if you ever get corsetted together with me some day!

MABIE presses up against PENNY's torso with 'OG's tail.

BEATIFICA: Penny? Penny. Is that you?

They startle. All hide except for MABIE. PENNY hides behind MABIE's torso. BEATIFICA comes in and out of the room, getting dressed.

MABIE: No ma'am. I'm...just a ...friend of Penny's. She'll be right back.

BEATIFICA: Is Penny almost done. She's been here all day. I can hear her out there...dragging her feet...a soft thump...

MABIE: I was helping her clean and I was...

BEATIFICA *[Putting on lipstick, realistic]:* Well I'm sure she told you there's no dust here really, but I have her dust for me and just a little dog hair. Not bad for a college education, sweeping up some tufts of dog hair, ah?

MABIE: Good thing you bought that dog or Penny wouldn't have a summer job or half an education! *[Laughs]*

BEATIFICA: What?

MABIE: What kind of dog is it?

BEATIFICA: Tell her that I'm going back to work now. I don't want a raucous while I am gone.

MABIE: Oh no....

BEATIFICA: Walk the dog and bring in the mail. Or he'll be cooped up all day.

MABIE: Don't worry.

BEATIFICA: I could take the dog I guess. To the studio audience. Up in the plane, I don't know. What?

MABIE: Nothing. You just look so perfect. I'm... sorry.

BEATIFICA: What?

MABIE: Are you...um...doing a televised appearance? I've seen you before up close. I've come right up to the TV glass to see how perfect you are. Your eyes so clear in the pixels. I don't remember anything you say but I know you must know so many things about the world because you are so...well... uncluttered with misgivings and your historical romance, I mean your journalism, I mean I know people say these sort of things to you all the time I'm sorry.

BEATIFICA [*Aside as she autographs something for MABIE*]: Yeah I hate that really...I never recognize you people but then [*She shudders*] "Cheerio, said the autograph, I'm just a squiggle, leave me alone. Don't let my husband crawl into bed thinking my maid is me."

MABIE: And I won't get the days mixed up when you come back and crawl in your bed with you.

BEATIFICA: Karl? Comere. You're coming with me.

BEATIFICA looks for dog at dog level. MABIE MAIN and PENNY attach themselves to BEATIFICA's torso with THE 'OG's castrated "tail." They walk her back into the bedroom in a state of near ecstasy.

DOLLY [*Jilted aside to SHIRLEY*]: You can striptease in a pool stick powder blue for the Nantucket Muffin Shop to stay in shape and get yourself some quarters for the juke box.

Nicole Lowrance as Shirley with The 'Og (PS122)

Coin #4: Darts at the Breast

THE 'OG gets thrown out to sea, and foists a Faustian dilemma onto SHIRLEY in the glass-bottomed boat. DOLLY treads water behind them, eavesdropping.

SHAGGY'OG: Since you're on your way—

SHIRLEY: To Hell?

SHAGGY'OG: Yes.

SHIRLEY: Well?

SHAGGY'OG: Do you hear that sort of breathless flute?

SHIRLEY: It's my breath, giving up my ghost.

SHAGGY'OG: I'd like a recording.

SHIRLEY: Nice. I used to know a girl who'd be absent from school to play the "recorder" and I didn't get it until later that it's the same thing as those sort of black box ones stuck in the wreck of a small plane!

SHAGGY'OG: Small of the back is how we tell that joke.

SHIRLEY: Don't say that when we're airborne—

SHAGGY'OG: Where I'm from?

SHIRLEY: Where I'm from.

SHAGGY'OG [*Wink*]: ...Thou to the pilot.

SHIRLEY: You're just losing your head again.

SHAGGY'OG: Yes, I'm drifting...Is it you? Or am I still above you?

SHIRLEY: Pull it back down like a kite. You'll get clear shadows in that altitude.

SHAGGY'OG: You be me.

They burlesque each other with the swaying of the boat.

SHAGGY'OG: You have the nape of a swan you know. They say a woman's glory is her nape and I see yours glowing at your... halo filling up your voice. You could predict the weather or the Lottery. And, oh, to dub you under the carnage of heads blown all to bits...yet voiced over clear. Small limbs imploded by a stepfather's hand or dragged from the back of a still-confederate pick-up truck. Necks strung global from the trees for this or that blaspheme of a sitcom guffaw. And now potentially, the riot to end all riots. If we can't agree you can skin me alive and have my brain suctioned dumb. For instance now, I'm such a fop that I would swing you 'til I split.

DOLLY: Oh please. Could you please.

SHIRLEY: Oh yes, I mean, um...

SHIRLEY unbuttons her blouse.

DOLLY: Peak-a-ba-boo that bosom little girl.

SHIRLEY: That is very fine.

DOLLY: Peek-a-ba-boo.

SHIRLEY: Pa-peek-a-ba-boo.

SHAGGY'OG: Where did it go, that little sucker.

DOLLY: Back to the damn darts on her blouse

SHAGGY'OG: Pa-peek-a-ba-boo.

SHIRLEY: Darted at me too—

DOLLY: Oh lean a little forward, baby, in them darts—

SHAGGY'OG: Easy on us baby... Oh that's hot.

DOLLY: Say peek-a-boo but not like—

SHAGGY'OG: Say it with your—yeah...

DOLLY: Oh, the other one.

SHAGGY'OG: Alright—

DOLLY: Alright—

SHIRLEY: Alright...

Coin #5: Tusk Marx

SHIRLEY, DOLLY & THE 'OG drift past MABIE who has been hogtied like a buoy and thrown into the sea. MABIE exposes a tusk in the wooing of THE 'OG tying it back to her tragic daughter Pilar, counter-wooing with her own revolutionary preaching.

MABIE: Oh no. Watch out!

SHIRLEY: What?

DOLLY: What?

SHIRLEY: What happened? Mommy?

MABIE: He's got a tusk! I saw it! Oh don't pull her down to Hellgate like Pilar! He's got a tusk in every word.

SHIRLEY: What tusk? Who is Pilar?

DOLLY: Where did you see a tusk?

MABIE: I overheard it in his voice! There was a tusk in every word!

DOLLY: Oh no you're wrong, Mabie. He's right. I finally understand what he's been preaching all along. And Coney Island is a joke. We won't go back there, Curly, we'll resist the great burlesquing of our over-the-counter unskilled labor that's not even worth its ink on an application form. To the Devil with these so-called traumatic realisms that prove nothing but corporate mirroring, pop logic. Pshaw. There is no "behind" to the signs we've been assigning all along. We been stripteased by the gover'ment, down to the Red by which we jump at

DOLLY [cont'd]: chances and to conclusions like they're bones! And everything we say is just a pithy paraphrase of ribbitry. But Shirley, if we locate...in ourselves a concealed weapon that will spur us from inferiority into colossal torsos of...a time when.. oh...If you don't marry him, Shirley, I'll scalp your head and dress up as you and...jump his bones.

SHIRLEY: Oh Mom, you say such awful things. I think he's married that tycoon that's swooned already.

SHAGGY'OG: And from such an intimate positioning [as I long intended], I will bring the system down around its ears. Perhaps this is the key. Divorce the tycoon and run off with the revolution! Hm.

MABIE: I'm telling you this is the very boy that turned my Pilar's head with hope and hype he dug out of pamphlets and cranked into her like caffeine! I hear it in his tusks. What did he say to get her curly head so riled up?

SHIRLEY: Curly hair? Oh no! Pilar!

MABIE: Pilar wrote, "Mama, there's a typhoon coming that is manmade. You must surrender to its power. It will wash away the porn and grit of New York City and the world wide web. It will bring the skyscrapers to their knees." Poor Pilar. She treaded water from this very spot where she could see that tycoon picture window. My Pilar...knew what to do with that tusk. Didn't she, Karl?

SHIRLEY: What did she do with it? Who is Pilar?

DOLLY: I change my mind. Let's rip his tusk out of him once and for all.

SHIRLEY: Okay then, hack it off I guess, I mean...um! Wait...

DOLLY: Let's poke his eye out with his own tusk, come on honey—

SHIRLEY: I see what you're saying, mom. And I hear Aunt Mabie's dialectics also but I've written something for myself just now. Maybe it will be a swan song and—

DOLLY: No, Shirley!

MABIE: Curly!

SHIRLEY: Neither one of you can mother me forever, Mom. And Mabie, I will come upon a moment where I could entusk myself and leave this song behind, I don't know. I'm all confused tonight.

SHAGGY 'OG: Your thoughts are swarming at our eardrums like mosquitoes of the soul, dear, go ahead.

SHIRLEY: I feel like I've received an education that will turn me to...computers...in the long run. Or to endlessly shampoo in some salon. Hm, that sort of rhymes. So here it is, okay...I think it's called "Red Sheath"— *[She clears her throat]*

SHAGGY 'OG: Dear God. It's taken place without us. Look at that.

BEATIFICA and PENNY float by on a sunken glass-bottomed, single-engine plane with a great "tusk" sticking out of BEATIFICA's torso. Dreadful pause.

Coin #6: Slapstick Floggings of the Real Sublime

BEATIFICA and PENNY on their way to Hell have been entusked mysteriously in MABIE's sudden revolution. MABIE mourns for PENNY, and THE 'OG mourns for BEATIFICA. THE 'OG strips down to an ancient and colossal torso, demanding the flogging of BEATIFICA and PENNY to see if they are just disguising themselves as ghosts in order to escape the revolution. MABIE gets reduced to a website by her blind outrage.

BEATIFICA *[Aria-like, entusked]*:

I have gone to your water carousel in winter

Jostled and jounced inside its tidal wave

I rode it high back to th'aquarium

Beside the elephant large as a church

I looped the loop, I shot the chutes

I whirled in the tilt-a-whirl-a-somersault

To where the girls will always have laps to fall back on, tunnel of love 'n five cent trolley smile

Wonderwheel of ten cent chaos.

And the water camel lifts his hump

For me to ride-a-go-round-awhile

Pockets fall away,

shoot at the tin rabbits and the coral flames of

BEATIFICA [cont'd]: Hell in an electric bathing suit

   Kiss the surface from below

   Where my foot used to mark its urban pressure

   Clothed in my right mind long ago.

   The slot in the machine bestows its glare, glare everywhere and nowhere there a shadow

   for the Whichaway Coins a nickel arcade

   Pick the gray one in the razzle dazzle glass box.

   Do you know why?

   The creatures travel in a carousel like this?

   Touch the glass they scatter to confusion.

   Out of season, rock and roar.

PENNY: *Don't feed the Lions your lit cigarettes*

   Don't rock and roar the gray people please

   Don't drive the cold-blooded back to the corners of their cages with a will-o'-the-wisp.

   Don't stand up on the leap frog railway with a head full of dread.

SHAGGY 'OG: Or some new pink aquarium in your eye.

DOLLY [*Near tears*]: I miss the Wonderwheel! Oh Shirley, take me back to feeling good about myself.

SHIRLEY: You know he has an okay body but I don't like how he talks when he gets dressed.

SHAGGY 'OG [*Turning disgust onto DOLLY & SHIRLEY*]: Poor little stadium of piano ears come out to overhear the execution of straw labor. Aha tragedy repeated into farce. I'd love to see the pith beat out of that.

MABIE: Baathist terror, Mao surveillance, cranked up napalm. Fist of Tito, eeny meeny, slogan here and who will it be? Sent home in a body bag with a bill for the bullets.

SHIRLEY: Just a minute and then we'll walk out. Okay?

DOLLY: Before they send the offering plate around.

SHIRLEY: We'll get our things together, your purse, your coat, and sneak out the back, okay?

DOLLY: I know, but don't forget to snatch his secret little oil can.

SHIRLEY: That's funny mom. That's the funniest joke I've ever heard.

DOLLY: But it's a private joke. Shh. Don't tell anyone.

SHIRLEY: Where is it, in his costume?

DOLLY: It isn't trivia, honey, it is the Greeks.

SHAGGY 'OG [*About BEATIFICA's real body*]: She is still lifelike is she not? And still beloved? Am I right? Am I right?

DOLLY: She ain't lifelike, not to me.

SHIRLEY [Feeling 'OG's real torso]: I'd say she ain't either, hm...but you...

SHAGGY 'OG: We saw eye to eye a few times.

DOLLY: Now you seem the more lifelike, I'd go on record as saying, but I tend to identify more with— I don't root for the female torso, yeah...it's weird, I know—

SHIRLEY: He's Olympic nearly, Mama, with his shirt off. That's what drew me to him. See?

DOLLY: Bit more work in the gymnasium and there'd be muscle!

SHIRLEY: Rippled sort of—

DOLLY: Flexing...

SHIRLEY: Hardcore—

DOLLY: Oh it is hard.

SHIRLEY: Oh. But softer to the pinch and peak-a-boo. [She pinches him]

"Opera Glasses"

Burlesque curtain: BEATIFICA slowly serves PENNY with a serving tray. MABIE MAIN eavesdrops. A player piano plays from a distance.

Stacey Karen Robinson as Mabie (PS122)

BEATIFICA: Do you wish to feel more...

PENNY: Buoyant?

BEATIFICA: Yes. Flamboyant even.

PENNY: Long ago I had a buoyancy, but now—

BEATIFICA: Can I get you anything? Your opera glasses?

PENNY: Everything.

BEATIFICA: Can I bring you—

PENNY: All of it.

BEATIFICA: Can I dress you?

PENNY: And undress my feet—Be still.

BEATIFICA: I won't break anything of yours that was mine

PENNY: I want to see what lies ahead.

She stands, tentatively, on Beatifica's face.

BEATIFICA: Here it is.

BEATIFICA hands her the opera glasses, "tusk," from her spine placed neatly on her tray.

PENNY: Put it away.

BEATIFICA: You seemed to want it—

PENNY: I don't want it.

BEATIFICA: Oh Penny. I remember it vaguely as a sort of tusk. On the mantle. There came a day when there it was, a replica of my heirloom mass-produced and affordable. Karl himself could afford it and then what? How could we look across the sea at eventide.

PENNY: Just say evening. It's not worth the accent. Do you intend to handle what is mine, as Karl did yours?

BEATIFICA: When I am with you—

PENNY: When I'm not there—

BEATIFICA: Just to put it back—

PENNY: To put it on your tray? And then what? Then what?

BEATIFICA: You'll keep watching with your naked eye to see what I will do with it, in the corner of your eye. You won't even think of it until I do. At the same time—

PENNY: And you'll raise it to your face...

BEATIFICA: In the olden days maybe—

PENNY: Who was it at the helm of this revolt?

BEATIFICA [*Looking into the "tusk"; she bows again, underneath her tray*]: My service. Oh Penny, my tray.

MABIE [*Pulls PENNY down into her hiding place*]: We would need pure action from you, Penny, not this sort of lifeless support. We can tell you see Beatifica's dialect now for what it is, in retrospect of course. Transfusing your comprehension of practical materials. We knew she'd gotten so surplussive from the superstructure that we leant to you and frankly, when you noticed crucial shifts in point of view from 1st person plural to 3rd person plural "people" that was my voice speaking to you through the torso's pamphlets and I take a singular verb as a collective pronoun. How is the dream elite, you ask? We ask our cell of selves. How is the science or psychology [*She spits*] of it not elite? Are we not entitled to our opiates of guns and roses? As we stroke at each other calling it mutual use. Calling it demand. Calling it exchange. Calling it movement. The pulp doled out to us by the very last means of production is an obsolete

MABIE [cont'd]: torso anointed for us to screw and bolt. The Torso Marxists from the stone age of their industry once offered muscle when there was steel and a railroad to be built, Meanwhile you go off to cyberpunkdom and from there publish secondary sources in second person You You You your paltry points of view pointing the finger to mobilize me now for what? Another backfired, shortsighted error that did not predict counter-revolutionary terror? When is there NOT counter-revolutionary terror? When is there not the side effect of massacre to invert the order? We wield the torso as a tool itself. We don't exactly quote him like he's got some deified solidarity on our indigenous catastrophes. He was a Eurocentric bastard pawn of a dagger. Now our tools are of the mind—the production of the mind as a machine.

SHIRLEY and DOLLY poke out their heads.

SHIRLY GOODNESS: Except for me because I flunk your questionnaires and go to the mall.

DOLLY: But we're behind you all the way in terms of voting yes.

SHAGGY 'OG [*Breaking the fourth wall viciously into the studio audience—a new typhoon*]: I call now for the flogging of these gods again! They won't feel anything if they are really gods. Here now. At the lip of the stadium!

PENNY: Can you see through the ceiling as to what is at the helm of this purgatorio, please? Now please?

SHAGGY 'OG: Closed Caption for the Real Sublime: A life-like torso Antinoos beloved of the Emperor Hadrian who died in the flower of his youth in 4th Century B.C. was not lifelike by anatomical correctness which we learned in the Renaissance when god became man but lifelike by belovedness, you see. A sovereignty that must be razed to the ground. Right now! I call for that!

SHIRLEY: Let's get out of here.

DOLLY: Okay.

They exit discreetly. A curtain is partially drawn.

SHAGGY'OG [*Breaking the fourth wall even more viciously*]: I call now for the flogging of these gods again! They won't feel anything if they are really gods. Here now. At the lip of the stadium. Shall be a slapstick flogging of the Real Sublime. And then we'll see what's slapstick and what's real once and for all. When we burst open each proscenium to weigh its impact. Its belovedness. We'll see which one is coined once and for all. We'll see red. I want to see real red right now. And that's the difference.

MABIE: Aha. You're angry. You disrobe yourself of all your platforms into blind rage in the end. Flex your six-pack abs of infomercial bullshit.

SHAGGY'OG: Yes I'm angry and you're not, why is that, do you think? Fuck you women's libbers. I can still buy pornography of you fucked up the ass and be court jester in this day and age, live like a king.

MABIE: Fuck the muscle of the eye. The muscle of the nerve. The muscle of the breast, that colonial milkmaid organ. The sinew of imagination. We shall educate ourselves to speculate rather than to correct. If there be such correction that has all the sciences in its fist and the raw materials in its leapfrogging thigh. Or maybe I'm just another fragment of a woman running from the ancient stadium with no belovedness at all.

SHAGGY'OG [Stark naked but for the tusk]: YOU BLASPHEME THE CREED!!!!!

THE 'OG brutally hits MABIE MAIN in the mouth.

MABIE: If it were comprehensible rhetoric I wouldn't profane it. If I'm sitting in my factory all day long how can I grasp the footnotes and cross references of the ruthless critique of everything existing with my hands on the factory knobs? You'll always outwit me so go ahead you bastard Shakespeare evangelical. De Ja Vu Ad hominum blackmail. The white regret is just part of the catch-22. And I refuse to be sprung from the brain of any Greek statuary. I've joined the Iraq Liberation Action Committee. I didn't think Sayid Kadhom Al-Battat should have been beaten like that at the turn of the century by the Turkish officials on his way back from a New York downtown theatre to Baghdad where they have three universities that teach torture and rape as patriotism and where a death sentence was waiting for him on July 19, 2001. I thought it should have been on the news. I don't know why we don't hear about these things.

MABIE runs, faster and faster and then leaps into the air. Her legs slowly petrify into salt, a fragment of a ruin. A piece of her hardens and a lovely sheath comes over it hearing the insignia: "www.liberateiraq.org."

set design by Juman Malouf

Coin #7: From Beside Herself

BEATIFICA and PENNY speak in a newly revolutionized hierarchy where the first shall be last. BEATIFICA serves PENNY a sort of tusk that seems to have been, at one time, heirloom opera glasses. A curtain is partially drawn shut even more, player piano music.

PENNY: Well I see. Can you sing?

BEATIFICA: I used to hum.

PENNY: Can you dance?

BEATIFICA: I used to swoon.

PENNY: What can you do with any excellence?

BEATIFICA: Calligraphy perhaps. I have reams and reams of it.

PENNY: A ridiculous apprenticeship. Ornate curlicues with nothing in them. No peach. Still life.

BEATIFICA: Deep in the insignia there are hemispheres of vengeance just like yours. I try to improve my calligraphy all day. There are strugglemarks on the walls where I have dragged things heavy and cursed under my breath with no strong arm to haul these things for me.

PENNY: Do you have any support anywhere now? Or will you be leaning on my footing for that?

BEATIFICA: I have none. I have no support anywhere.

PENNY: Are you still in love with the torso's hand? The one you thought had a gentleness as it rested on the piano or beside a plate of food he carved for you?

BEATIFICA: It seems to have thickened now, thrashing in the sea, set apart from itself.

PENNY: You knew it was thick, that it would always be thick.

BEATIFICA: It had a blunted force. Hammering at my will.

PENNY: It can still shape its students with one welt of flotsam to the brow.

BEATIFICA: Are they equal tones now that it plays? All the red and white keys?

PENNY: I refuse to speak with you on any historical subject. You are inferior to me politically. Your family is ignorant. You are the thorn of any paradisio, breaking the will of the lesser ones like a stadium chair splayed open on the spine of a smaller spine, wanting your holiday.

BEATIFICA: You stand still in a place beside the proletariat.

PENNY: You're not divine, that's final now. You seem the same. Death is the same and I'm the same. I am beside myself.

Coin #8: Red Sheath

DOLLY and SHIRLEY reflect on SHIRLEY's home-schooled education while watching MABIE's leaping legs erode underwater in the aquarium at Coney Island.

DOLLY: Yeah. I feel like I'm much less of an authority figure for you, Shirley, if we breathe in all these ancient vapors on our field trips, does that bother you?

SHIRLEY: I kinda miss the syndicated part.

DOLLY: I really like your... "Red Sheath for the Modern Revolutionary" idea that you were going to read when you cleared your throat awhile back. I'd like to encourage...well the part about the..."oh the hilt, the hilt again please, here where it would lock, it unlocks." Until that part I thought it was just pulp...you know, but as long as we get to a point where everything's redundant in the sort of realism of it, we'll be okay. We like these sort of things...It made me want to...

SHIRLEY: Have me all to yourself?

DOLLY: We can do that. We can think up anything—

SHIRLEY: So you think I changed my ways? From then on?

DOLLY: Well no, I guess I made it all larger than life-sized...I don't know where these things come from. I don't know who is speaking to me most of the time.

SHIRLEY: I'll just speak to you from now on, okay? We'll be together. Just the two of us.

DOLLY: Okay.

SHIRLEY: Are you okay?

DOLLY: Yeah. Are you?

SHIRLEY: Yeah.

DOLLY: Good. That's good.

Epilogue

SHIRLEY's poem when she cleared her throat while sitting in the glass-bottomed boat...

"Red Sheath for the Modern Revolutionary Peking Romance"

By the flames of fury burning in your breast plate red / you carved a sword to cut through grasses of knives and iron dead/ You pledged your hatred to bruise the chains that/bound you to a Bottomless stain of centuries eye for eye and blood for blood. /When I commanded you to lay your weapons down, You turned toward my whisper, blade awash with lightning/Rage uncircumcized where you could bury me alive/In jaded dragons that would melt like ice against your fist/You would protect me then here at my scabbard collar/Here at my plaited sleeve, here at the tassels of my thigh/ Here at the brasses of my throat, you'd braid me loosely into you/Then, tugging at my backstrap knots yanked right/Against the storm that would unfurl me to my full length/As in the arching of your foot, that arches back my spine /That tapers us toward the tip, serrating slightly now /Now scalloped, now so sharply struck, fit to the very womb / Of pommels, lacquered now...engraving lightly / At my softest ridges with your name in gilt chrysanthemums / Worn down like leather slipping in a thrust of / Waists ungirded to the underside of our suspended mounts / Now galloping and leaping, touching ground and hooves/Reared into sand, now springing to the clasp so tiny at the—/Oh, the hilt—the hilt again please—here where it would lock/It unlocks, oh, it thrashes us away, flung down and weeping/Where it's, ah, so binded to the double-edg'ed-edge.../we'd weep the porcelains to silk, gunpowder into tea and wash the waters still and clear and deep...

Nina Hellman, photo: BobHandelman.com

~ END OF RED FROGS ~

STADIUM DEVILDARE:

Battle for GdzillaX,

a new reality program for an American war zone

by

Ruth Margraff

Introduction to Stadium Devildare – Part A

By Rich Werner, Co-Director

      In one of my emails to Ruth from 2006 I said I wanted our production of STADIUM DEVILDARE to "create the illusion of great space in a tiny space." I imagined this could happen with a revolving sit n' spin platform to mark changes in time and place; a skateboard ramp for race and chase scenes, hiding and tomb; and with Crenshaw & Lamar's explosives store built like a rolling lemonade stand. The motorcycle design went through many sketches of half-hobby horse with half-body puppet welding about which I wrote: "I may use them all." My sound design ideas read almost like a poem to help demonstrate how the character is transforming into something "other than human":

> *Sound of starter pistol*
>
> *Sound of a knife being thrown through the air, traveling in slow motion and hitting its target*
>
> *Like Blue only slower*
>
> *Sad tune to be whistled*
>
> *Acapella vocal interludes*
>
> *Godzilla's unmistakeable roar. LOUD; War drums played simultaneously with live drums LOUD*
>
> *Buzz of a tattoo machine—to barely above a whisper*
>
> *Dubbed martial arts videogame punch and kick sound*

      My theater NOTE is one of Los Angeles' few democratically run theatre ensembles and it is amazing to me how many of these ideas got realized in our production with a fairly modest budget. We saw an excellent opportunity in Ruth's play to stage a highly theatrical, multi-media ensemble work, relevant to our times because the play touches on themes of pop culture and media manipulation so near to the heart of American culture. Karen Jean Martinson and I worked with Ruth for over a year via internet from Los Angeles while Ruth lived between Greece, New York City and Chicago. We expanded her text to fit a larger group of actors than the earlier 2004 Rude Mechanicals, Austin, TX production. We also brought in writer/composer Joshua Fardon to create and perform an original live score to the work. Mask, magic, puppet, Pilates, and Martial arts workshops were given to help our performers prepare.

By the time the show opened in February of 2008 we had a quasi-operatic sci-fi, cutting-edge panto complete with ninja cheerleaders, giant monsters, destroyed cities sculpted out of foam, an Evil Knievel and Elvis' hybrid clone, Lone Wolf Reiko's howl, and the Dazzlers' treachery. And, in keeping with the world and my original email daydreams—there was plenty of merchandise sold in the Lobby. Oh yes. And Godzilla, of course.

Richard Werner is a long-time ensemble member of Theater of Note, an actor, performance artist and theatre maker who lives and works in Hollywood CA. He graduated from SUNY New Paltz, guest stars on numerous TV shows and is the founder/producer of the annual Hollywood Performance Marathon now in its 17th year.

Introduction to STADIUM DEVILDARE – Part B

By Karen Jean Martinson, Ph.D.,
Dramaturg and co-director

I hear you howling, Lone Wolf Reiko. More than that, I feel your cry; its solitude pierces me, cuts to my heart until I can no longer bear it and I too tilt my head back, look to the moon, and scream out. Can you hear me, Reiko? Do you hear yourself in me?

As theatre artists, we constantly do battle, but we are scarred. Similar to the world of Ruth Margraff's STADIUM DEVILDARE: *Battle for G*dzilla X (a new reality program for the American arena)*, it often seems like we fight against glossy avatars. Perhaps we feel this more acutely in Hollywood, where small theatres operate in shadows cast by the flickering images of the big screen. Doe-eyed beauties of romantic comedies, unbreakable warriors of action films, 3D animated dogs and bears are all crassly pulled from the bins of nostalgia. Not to mention the figures who populate primetime dramas and sitcoms, or the competitions, exploitations, and debauchery of Reality TV. So large and so bright, those looming faces look like us. Sometimes they even are us. They do something that seems akin to what we do, and yet they live a world away and at cross-purposes to us. They literally lack substance. Still, they dominate our cultural landscape. They divert our collective attention, and they devour our time, energy and resources.

STADIUM DEVILDARE effectively queries the overbearing spectacle that marks our cultural moment and puts what is a disembodied, elusive, and oh-so-hard-to-put-a-finger-on conflict center stage. As it becomes physicalized, its social and political ramifications are made evident. Entertainment, distraction, fear, and warfare blend together to become the guiding ethos of The Stadium, where military and capitalist interests unite to market warfare as entertainment and nationalist pride. This arena—sponsored by the Special Forces Counter Militia—conflates pop culture with national defense, violent confrontation with patriotism, greed with national pride, and American imperialism with style.

As fantastical as The Stadium is, it is only a half-step away from our contemporary reality. Through the act of deciphering STADIUM DEVILDARE (or to use the language of the text—creating our own cheatcodes that would guide the storytelling of our production), we were struck by how the play uses spectacle to critique spectacle. STADIUM DEVILDARE creates an event that mimics the images and rhetoric of

American Exceptionalism, militarism, and entertainment – Stars & Stripes, Guts'n'Glory, All American Patriotic Fireworks. We become swept away by the excitement and the dream. Yet in its more pensive moments, the play allows us to see the underbelly to this fantasy: the labor required to uphold the façade; the toll it takes on those who must maintain it; the violence it seeks to recast, diffuse, or mask.

In our staging, we attempted to reveal the resonances between the fictional world of The Stadium and the real world of the United States under the latter years of the Bush Administration, hoping to remind the audience that we indeed exist in a moment of war and crisis. By emphasizing the raucousness of the competition and only gradually escalating its danger and the trauma it inflicts, we strove to make audience members complicit in the story – first its fun and then its horror. So that, like the characters who inhabit this world, we each must decide whether to engage in the game, to follow its rules, or to find a means of resistance.

Karen Jean Martinson is a theatre scholar, dramaturg, director, and sometimes puppeteer who is proud to have staged works from Minneapolis to Mexico to Chicago to Los Angeles. Martinson was awarded her Ph.D. in Theatre History, Literature, and Critical Theory from the University of Minnesota in 2008. Through her academic research, teaching, and artistic work, she explores contentious issues of race, class, gender, and sexuality within USAmerican consumer culture, utilizing theatre as the means through which greater social, political, and cultural insight can be perceived, expressed, debated, and enacted. She currently teaches Theatre at Chicago State University and spends most of her time researching and writing about El Vez, The Mexican Elvis. She also knits, does yoga, and rides her bicycle whenever she can.

STADIUM DEVILDARE:

Battle for GdzillaX,

a new reality program for an American war zone

by

Ruth Margraff

Production History

STADIUM DEVILDARE was first published in the Kendall/Hunt Publishing Company textbook *Performing The Here And Now: An Introduction To Contemporary Theater And Performance* ISBN: 0-7575-2085-5 edited by Chris Danowski Copyright: 2005.

STADIUM DEVILDARE was commissioned by the **Rude Mechanicals** premiering April 22 – May 22, 2004 at the Off Center **(Austin, Texas)**, funded in part by the *TCG/Metlife Extended Collaboration Grant* and an *NEA Creativity Fellowships and Services to Arts Organizations & Artists*.

Director: Shawn Sides

Composer: Graham Reynolds

Shawn Sides……………..Narrator

Jason Liebrecht…………Game Boy

Lana Lesley………………..Reiko

Joey Hood……………Crenshaw

Robert S. Fisher……………..Lamar

Photography by: Brett Brookshire, Lighting: Brian Scott; Costumes: Leslie Bonnell; Set Design: Stephen Pruitt; Sound: Robert S. Fisher;

An excerpt "Night Parachute Battalion" was translated into Romanian by Andreea Iacob for the **ManInFest International Journal of Teatrul Impossibil** 2005 and published by *Connotation Press, Issue III, Volume 1 Drama: November 2009*. "Night Parachute Battalion" was a finalist for the 10-minute play contest and produced at the **Actors Theater of Louisville**/Apprentice Co. Winter Showcase at the Bingham Theatre in Kentucky January 10-13, 2006 and at **Sweet Cantatas Festival/Sanctuary Playwrights' Theater** in Brattleboro, Vermont May 1-4, 2008.

STADIUM DEVILDARE's West Coast premiere February 15 –March 23, 2008 at **Theatre of Note (Hollywood/LA, CA)**

Directors: Rich Werner & Karen Jean Martinson, Music: Joshua Fardon

Jonathan Klein….Game Boy   Hiwa Bourne……Reiko

Justin Brinsfield……..Crenshaw   Jennifer Ann Evans……Lamar

Sofie Calderon….Narrator Lolly; Elizabeth Liang….Narrator Lolly2 David Bickford….Narrator/Waki; Sarah Lilly…Waki 2Lisa Clifton….Lolly extra, Rich PierreLouis…..Dazzler extra, Gina Garcia Sharp…Lolly extra; Producers: Stewart Skelton & Rich Werner; Lighting Design: Emily Eudy; Costume Design: Joel Scher & Gray Creasy; Graphic Designs by David Croy; Sound Design: Dennis Yen; Prop/Puppet Design: Gray Creasy & Rich Werner; Fight Choreographer: Marz Richards; Movement Choreographer: Michele Spears; Video Production: Darrett Sanders & Rich Werner; Stage Manager: Monroe Makowsky; Special Set Piece Designs by Brian O'Conner Jenny Nissenson, Josh Mohr & Erin Brewster; Dramaturg: Karen Jean Martinson; Marketing Committee Head: Hiwa Bourne

STADIUM DEVILDARE's Chicago premiere January 17 - February 24, 2013 at **Red Tape Theater (Chicago)** James D. Palmer, Producer

Director: Karen Yates

Lyndsay Kane….Narrator   Nicholas Combs….Game Boy

Carrie Drapac……Reiko   Andy Lutz……..Crenshaw

Matt David Gellin……Lamar

Stadium Fighters…Bryan Bosque, Sabrina Conti, Julian Hester, Mark Penzien, Nicole Rudakov, Derek Van Barham, Understudy: Paige Sawin; Mike Mroch (Set) Izumi Inaba (Costumes), Jacob Bray (Lighting), Chelsey Shilling (Projections), Casey Shillo (Props), Rachel Spear (Sound), Greg Poljacik (Fight Choreography), Paige Sawin (Asst Director), Molly Mullen (Dramaturg), Majel Cuza (Prod Mgr), Jarrod Bainter (Tech Dir)

Author's Notes:

The structure of this play is inspired by the deductive eliminations of popular TV reality programs. The characters have traces of Japanese anime characteristics in their behavior, which become more pronounced when they are rebellious, or more patriotic when they are favored by the game. The content has traces of reality by proxy to actual war zones erupting across war "theaters" with seemingly invisible eliminations and deductions in reality. *NOTE: TAKESHIS are written to be highly competitive obstacle contest interludes much like the pop TV series in Japan *Takeshi's Castle* where volunteers run gauntlets against **(use as directed)**: ghoulies, wrecking balls, platforms and pink trains, giant hand suits across numbered tiles, giant dominoes collapsing, cylinders across pool of water, wipeout on surfboards over fake whales, dashes through doors, dodgeball on balance beam, quake with wigs, karaoke, rice bowl downhill water slide, Velcro fly with wings and water, giant pinball, honeycomb maze, roller derby, wet paint spinning board up slippery slope, mushroom trip with giant mushrooms, tug of war, sumo rings, ride the wave, big bird elevated over stuffed rabbit, die or pie, yellow brick road, boulder dash, etc.

Special thanks to Graham, Shawn, Rich, both Karens, James, JohnnyO, Erik Ehn and Richard Emmert via Theatre Nohgaku, Fred Ho, Jose Figueroa, Susan Sontag, George Orwell, Christopher Crenshaw, Josef Dan Prall, Yukio Mishima's *Patriotism*, Koushun Takami's *Battle Royale*, Julie Regan for making my Evel Knievel lunchbox dreams come true, and Nikos Brisco always.

Roles:

All characters wear red, white and blue with their ranking emblazoned, as if competing gladiator style in a reality program set in an actual war zone.

NARRATOR—*dressed like a small-town beauty queen; avatar of reality control*

GAME BOY, Ranked #1—*First winner of Supraknievel status, makes an alliance with REIKO. Has a slightly Speed-Racer cartoon innocence but little is known about him other than his screen-name Palaiologoi and incredible luck for winning*

LONE WOLF REIKO, Ranked #2—*Anime changeling. Wears a red, white and blue tricentennial mini-dress. Her great uncle was Haruo Nakajima, stuntman inside original Godzilla suit 1954-1972. She can camouflage herself as a lower level Lolly painted to look Pokemon-six years old*

DAZZLER EXPO CRENSHAW, Ranked #4—*A gifted patriot, highly trained in pyrotechnics F/X and smuggling weapons grade explosives, ultimately wins the most important game piece –remastered from Evel Knievel era 1970s American daredevils to upset GAME BOY's ranking*

DAZZLER SPEED RACER LAMAR, Ranked #5—*A gifted patriot, disposable. Traffics in crashing into things at high speeds if people don't think his friends are cool. Never thought Crenshaw would go rent out the Suit to foreign corporate interests*

(**"LITTLE TEXIE"** Ranked #3—*an actual child, who writes invisible prophecies— never shows up on stage.*)

Jason Liebrecht as Game Boy (Rude Mechanicals, Austin)

Scene 1: START

"Reality Control"

The NARRATOR introduces the game. Inside the stadium, combatants battle for the first place prize—the SUPRAKNIEVEL suit of Guts'n'Glory. Combatants will ultimately face an actual war zone, known by the code GdzillaX.

NARRATOR [*holding placard: Reality Control*]:

Ladies and Gentlemen: The United States Special Forces Counter-Militia is proud to present the final Five combatants who have been competing here in our reality stadium, as you may know, in prep tournaments from all over the world. They will advance now to spar in a bloodsport challenge finally against the bestial and radioactive Rogue Weapons System (known by the alias GdzillaX)—

[*placard: The Foe*]

—The Foe—that has been plaguing our American nation far too long. In ancient gladiator style, and based on polls from viewers like yourselves, we have relocated our most patriotic finale to one of America's actual war zones. In this regard, and in an undisclosed location, during these events you will witness five of your favorites battle to defeat each other for the highest honor of—

[*placard: The Prize*]

—The Prize—to win the patriotic suit of Supraknievel Guts'n'Glory—stitched in vintage ostrich leather.

NARRATOR *(cont'd):* This gamepiece armor and matching retro Parachute will go to the first prize winner of each contest. Last worn under the trademark Evel Knievel in Snake River Canyon.

[placard: The Rules]

Here are the Rules: Rule A. Each player will be granted soldier status. Training is endorsed and licensed—sometimes teleprompted—for entertainment value.

Rule B. The cheatcode for the actual war zone is… GdzillaX. Please note we will not make reference to the actual war zone hereinafter.

Rule C. Intelligence gathered from this experiment will be used to eliminate once and for all those adversarial cells seeking to corrupt the freedoms we enjoy today.

Rule D. The cheatcode for hysteric females glomming onto this game will be: Lolly girl.

Rule E. We will expect a prophecy, for which we'll interrupt our format, from LITTLE TEXIE, ranked No. 3, the Lolly of the Lollies, and an actual child who is not here yet as you might have noticed.

Rule F. *[fineprint fast]* The-Stadium-is -not – responsible-for-any-bodily-injury-death-or-seizure-in- the-event- of-any-unforeseen-catastrophe—

Here comes a Lolly now, juz kiddin, let it roar! Let's go! Please welcome our second ranked combatant, LONE WOLF REIKO, ranked No. 2, Fulbright scholar to Japan, where she trained in an obscure but brutal Ninja/Noh cheerleading troupe. Reiko has dubbed over many anime classic beasts and lovers into the all-American English tongue that we are using here tonight.

Scene 2. GOD-SHELF BUGLE

No. 2 ranked REIKO laments that her lover, GAME BOY, keeps on winning but The Supraknievel suit is changing him. REIKO foresees a Godzilla disaster.

Forward slashes [/] indicate overlapping dialogue.

REIKO: Hahah? *[with anime gasp, she moves angularly, as if animated]* Deep inside the monster—must be hot as hell and dark and lonely—piloting the suit. Deep inside the monster's face.

NARRATOR: Yeah! You gotta crush on Game Boy or is it just whoever's in the lead.

[quick focus onto GAME BOY, then away]

REIKO: Hahah? *[an anime gasp]* The maimed and dead we close our eyes against are part of who we are. The fluttering behind our eyes…when we return, get blurry, panty shot, one wolf, one howling! From a cuter, fiercer time. And bruises underneath the ice. A yell struck in the air. Kicked into some blood-misted house / … and—

NARRATOR: / Excuse me, Reiko Girl Woof, ranked No. 2, we need to remind you that our prophet Little Texie, ranked No. 3, is an actual child. Please don't say anything age inappropriate in your remarks.

REIKO: Hahah? And keep your eyes soft. If I turn to you, in any way. When the white sun splits the sky.

NARRATOR: You have about one minute left to wrap this up.

Lana Lesley as Reiko (Rude Mechanicals, Austin)

"By Day"

REIKO overdubs an anime outro.

REIKO: By day we...

> *[sound of anime dubbed smile]*

by morning...

> *[startled grunt as if waking up]*

daylight sort of

> *[growing sigh as if something rubbing its belly]*
>
> *[squeal of pain]*
>
> *[gasp at shaft of energy]*

...what we do by day, of course...

> *[strange chuckle, muted gasp]*
>
> *[scream of falling from great height]*
>
> *[grunt of exertion, hentai childbirth]*

and having come so swiftly...

> *[gasp]*

having come so swiftly...

> *[sound of small smile]*
>
> *[resigned exhalation]*

REIKO transforms herself into something bestial and sensual in a flash and then she is a waif again.

NARRATOR: And that was our local hentai whippersnapper also known as LONE WOLF REIKO, ranked No. 2. Sponsored in part by Double-Headed Dragon anime since she's dubbed over the voice of MegaRot and KilSpleen Lollies into English. Wishing we could dub whatever she just told us into English also but oh well. And now. Please welcome! Give. It. Up! For the real-life former ROTC demolition derby stepbrothers. They fight side by side in fireworks that go by all sorts of red white and blue pseudonyms online—they. Are. Gifted patriots who traffic in American explosives. Way to go DAZZLER EXPO CRENSHAW ranked No. 4 and DAZZLER SPEED RACER LAMAR ranked No. 5. And in the swanky corner, sparring here for your appreciation, remastered by the National Vinyl & Propane Archives and underwritten by the Spirit of '76 Casino Breweries, here for a retro motorcade!—GAME BOY SUPRAKNIEVEL ranked at No. 1! Let's see ya keep that title gorgeous!

TAKESHI #1: gauntlet ghoulies. GAME BOY wins despite sexual tension between him and REIKO.

NARRATOR: Right on Game Boy! And still hangin' onto last place status here's our stragglers—

CRENSHAW: Watch it.

NARRATOR: Okay well.

LAMAR: I go back to training. I'll be back.

NARRATOR: Never thought he'd win, now there's a threat.

LAMAR: When we get to brother versus brother, you'll find out who's got the Roman /candles in the sky

NARRATOR: And who would that be? Mr. Rocket-in-the-jockstrap?

LAMAR: You'll find me layin in the battle grass with one eye still peeled open. Watchin' the back of my man Crenshaw over there, my bro.

CRENSHAW: There you go.

NARRATOR: So you're aligning yourself with your—/uh….brother…is he….

LAMAR: In proximity to greatness, yeah, I'm gonna bend down to the places where them trophy muscles start to bulge. From there I'll see my red, white and blue in ostrich leather.

CRENSHAW: I'ma grab that Suit—he gonna rim the ass of greatness right here.

LAMAR: I aspire up to second place and stickin' closer than a brother. Is. My strategy.

CRENSHAW: I obtain the Suit and turn this numb nut crap around. That gives way to my crap and game over.

NARRATOR: This just in from our prophet Little Texie, ranked No. 3 who is an actual child. She has some hobbies in the way of joysticks, piloting, and bloodthirst—

REIKO: Ahem. The actual child is right now connecting to her fourth or fifth connecting flight and is actually delayed. But has submitted this prophecy she wrote herself which she asked that I deliver for her.

NARRATOR: Our little prophet, as I said, is an actual child, 5 years old, named Little Texie...

REIKO: You're repeating yourself.

NARRATOR: Has prophesied for us/ by twitter—

REIKO: An invisible prophecy by Little Texie. She sent it in like this, with the invisible ink an' all—

NARRATOR: Such a bright kid.

Scene 3. "TOY TEA"

A prophecy from the absent No. 3 ranked TEXIE, an actual child. Foretells GdzillaX Armageddon will defeat the suit of Guts'n'Glory.

REIKO [*reading the prophecy*]: TOY TEA...There will be a king of monstahs. Crushing the blue bonnet toy people tea. He is not a monstah. He is the king of monstahs.

TAKESHI #2: competitive roaring chorus.

There will be a king of monstahs...Roaring highly classified black plumes and lightning. As the sky itself! The sea itself is tearing! Towers shatter! Houses in contrailed exhaust! Shock waves underground. The blue bonnets scream in the garage. 'Til they're charred stumps to kick around. Rotting in the craw as the king of Monstah's sealevel Stomping comes down in a blackout. All the lamps and clocks and toy tea sets will come down in the blackout. With blue bonnet eyes crawling in the yard.

Sound of monster crushing a toy tea set.

"Camouflage"

REIKO [*genuinely upset, with hentai flourishes, misinterprets prophecy*] She's dead! I know it. Little Texie's dead. That's what she's foretelling. No pseudo-kid is just a child in this game. Look at their little eyes, those widescreen popups shimmering with fear, suspicion and veiled hatred. Fine hair fluffing in the breeze until it hardens into weaponry. Rarely played by actual kindergarten. Armed to the baby teeth with battle axes, penny Pods with laser trackers, hatchets halfway lodged in their little cartoon faces. Goo leaking out of batteries and razors flashing in their papercut mouths. They will turn us into the reality control. Why do you think the kids always wander down deserted streets? Or stumble into rusty, filthy holes? Or cages that are roaring? Why do they step into a tidal wave with nothing but a day-glow innertube?? Hopskotch up to some creep in a car by the playground, yeah, with that cold cup of coffee on the dashboard. They're so cute and fierce just aching for the fang to come along and suck the Sweet Honesty right out of the Avon angel that you get when you turn six.

NARRATOR: And now for some footage we can really download. Dressin' for success and feelin' fly. Hey No. 1 for Pay Dirt - Game Boy SupraKnievel! How. Does. It feel?

Costumes: Leslie Bonnell; Set Design: Stephen Pruitt (Rude Mechanicals, Austin)

Scene 4. MOTORCADE MIC

GAME BOY's acceptance speech, as he puts on the Suit of Guts'n'Glory, highly-prized game piece.

GAME BOY as SUPRA-KNIEVEL: Well first of all just let me thank my Lollies, I am standin in the shadow of your high school flag pole. I seen you put your right hands on your heart. You got the brightest flag to climb that pole.

And to the mamas, well I tried to sound like Elvis on your telescreen. To get ya'll on the back of my bike. I lifted up your bicentennial skirts in a perfect breeze for blowin' like a kiss across my stadium. But you know what? Nowadays we're gonna land on the float with the princess twirlers. We're gonna fly through the air and live in the sunlight.

And to them little boys that wanta be a soldier, I'm reaching for your flag unfurling. I watch you touch your lunch box where my face'll come to be—You busted up your dirt bike where the grass is growin' from the puddle to the swing an' I am grabbin' everything I learned from your survival. Cuz every pieceuh luggage can be built up like a parachute. We got yer office fortified Amerkan to spring back by the next business day. I got a plan for everything to be unstompable like me, from any big ole pig licker lizard.

And to the Daddies, we been foldin' all yer flags and sayin' nope to dope. We been honorin' the custody of them that reared up your delinquence.

GAME BOY *[cont'd]*: We been proud to be the longhorn son of a willie and pledged our allegiance to the ball, the puck, the pigskin. But now's the time to step up to the ramp America. You got the freedom not to feel too patriotic. You been squattin' on the soldier blood of somebody else's grandpapoose. Now's the time to gladiate for something more than just a snake pit derby you got off on growin' up.

"Crank Up the Diesel"

[rock anthem style]

GAME BOY: Crank up the diesel, blow it up. Toe to toe okay, ya hear me? Crank up the propane, blow it up! Can't keep wrasslin' Pepsi trucks laid end to end and pretty canyons nowadays, my lollies. Crank up the hydrogen and blow it up! Get 'em in between the nostrils. Crank up the gamma rad and blow it up. Get em in between the stompin' on the people for the people, by the people, we the people, Viva that! Far out lollies, this is gonna waste us all except for No. 1 and that be me, let's fuckin' go! Red White and Blue!

NARRATOR: Wow! And how's your golf swing.

GAME BOY: Like a handshake, sweetie.

NARRATOR: And your baby kissing?

GAME BOY: Ticklish.

NARRATOR: How did you get to where you are?

GAME BOY: Jumped the gun

Blows kiss & winks.

Scene 5. PYRO PATRIOTS

In their fireworks kinda outpost, LAMAR and CRENSHAW suck up to the Suit with "Century Pinwheels into Red Sky" explosives… REIKO surveils.

CRENSHAW: Respectin' your No. 1-ness, suh. We gotcha loaded up with fireworks tonight…We gotcha parachute battalions, six or seven on the bottle rocket lanterns, multi-shot, reloadable. You let us know okay/ you /yeah /yeah /yeah /yup/yaw

LAMAR:/Whistle fountains in the cobalt / century pyro pinwheel into red…/We gotcha fire flower in the sky

CRENSHAW: And and and ragin' alligator at the Battle of Orleans, a coupla cobra strikes (ole cracklin' favorites) and then you wanta maybe zig zag into triple fun or twitter glitter or just snare drum ammo into thunderclaw salute/or/or/ whut/ uh/ uh/

LAMAR: /Or. Or maybe plain smoke if you wanta vanish in a rockstar sorta lemon rodeo uh/ uh/ uh roman candles on the cake

CRENSHAW *[aside]:* You wanna quitcher blowin' on the godfather here or make me shave your cum beard that you're workin' so goddam hard on.

LAMAR *[aside]*: Stick your schtick man

CRENSHAW: Fight, fuck or bust a fifty.

GAME BOY: Juz...juz make it glorious.

CRENSHAW & LAMAR: No problem sir, no problem. Glory comin' up, that's right.

GAME BOY: Not too many whistles. Bangs are good.

CRENSHAW & LAMAR: More bangin', that's no problem. Comin' right up.

GAME BOY: Little bangs and big ones. All of that's allright.

LAMAR: S'all good.

CRENSHAW: You rule—

LAMAR: Will you shut up and let me finish subjugating both of us.

GAME BOY: Juz wake me up when the sun slides off the poker. It's slantin' in the backside of my brain.

TAKESHI #3: giant pinball: GAME BOY slides down behind his Knievel motorcycle.

"Gravel"

When the Dazzlers turn their backs, REIKO challenges GAME BOY in order to obtain the Suit and release him from its spell.

REIKO: So maybe right before you get your fix of spine compression, when you gitcher rib cage pokin' through your collarbone in some new angle, Mr. No. 1—

Draws her weapon: music.

GAME BOY: I needed ya ta to pick the dandelions til the Tru Green truck could spray the lawn with all them lovesick polka-dotted dogs.

Strikes her, they spar: music TAKESHI #4: velcro fly.

REIKO: Maybe you can get yourself repaired from any sequel. So there's no welt, no scar tissue. After this.

GAME BOY: Let it come to my arena. Let it roar. Let's go.

TAKESHI #5: honeycomb maze: REIKO winning, but now has to take on GAME BOY.

"Airborne"

DAZZLERS catch REIKO in the act of attempting alliance. They battle. Triple-teamed, REIKO loses.

REIKO: I breathe in flames. From thoughts stuck underwater burning

GAME BOY: I'm the silhouette above/ your shadow.

REIKO: *[a sort of prayer]* /Where the cedars still grow sleeve to sleeve,

GAME BOY: Two shadows paired/ across the morning,

REIKO: Flung through the/ darkness of old radio

GAME BOY: Across the pining/ wind.

REIKO: And having come so swiftly…

NARRATOR: We gotta panty shot and Dazzlers bone-crunch in the tearing wind. Flag-colored gravel—Dazzlers skin their knees. They bleed Red White and Blue—

CRENSHAW & LAMAR: Spread the cupcake!

REIKO: Minus you guys.

Triple-teamed REIKO loses, cries.

LAMAR: Don't get too pensive, Lolly. Gimme that hopeless vibe…

CRENSHAW: Don't humiliate the drill team, bitch.

"Exit Interview"

With loser REIKO, who goes undercover as a Lolly girl.

NARRATOR: Lone Wolf Reiko is deflated. Down for the count she gets her first humiliation here, we got a failure belly up..... How. Does. It feel. To lose against a—

REIKO: It sucks. It goes really fast and then that's it. It's over and you feel like you could have been on some other side of it.

NARRATOR: But you did throw weaker strikes and all your—efforts were in general less successful than your opponent. Almost reminded me of my own childhood, the tantrums you were throwing... I was a very strong toddler, playing so roughly with my monsters in the garage. But we should probably be interested in the winner, shouldn't we. We're trying to set up a word with him in just a minute here—

"Velocity Idol"

Narrator interviews winner GAME BOY. He dismisses the threat of GdzillaX and insults the Dazzlers.

NARRATOR: Oh well look't that a spray of rockets for our still No. 1 ranked idol!

GAME BOY guzzling a six pack

NARRATOR: Can we grab a little triumph from your angle, Supraknievel. What are these Little Texie rumors about GdzillaX being next? Have you ever felt more like an aggrieved yet still colossal giant? Than you do right now? Meaning. Are you just bombed yourself *(haha)* or is this going as you trained and planned.

GAME BOY: I don't plan or exercise. I collectively humiliate.

NARRATOR: I have no doubt you can promise vengeance / to any—

GAME BOY: Don't fall out of step with my parade. Is how I put it.

NARRATOR: Nice. We'll cut to the hype in that case.

GAME BOY: I am the hype.

NARRATOR: I mean we'll be cutting to your minions No. 4 and 5.

GAME BOY: Waste of media.

NARRATOR: How 'bout a streak of weakness!

GAME BOY: Get outta here before I bash your mic arm with a baseball bat.

Shawn Sides as Narrator and Director

NARRATOR sticks out her cigarette with non-mic arm; GAME BOY lights it, chivalrous.

Scene 7. NOSTRIL SABOTAGE

TAKESHI #6: dodge ball: DAZZLERS plot revenge.

CRENSHAW: *[aside]* We got nostril sabotage on the Lolly cream filled blooper F/X hate to say.

LAMAR: When I, um, said I'd be No. 2 to No. 1 you know. I didn't mean to that bumpin' perv.

CRENSHAW: Bottom line I'd stoop down to your level but it'd be all balls & chin

LAMAR: Hey. Keep up the bliss on your end, bro

CRENSHAW: Or whut you gonna pump my donut in the parkin lot?

"Royal Blue"

Undercover as a Lolly, REIKO cons the dazzlers out of sparklers, which will lure the now-passed-out-drunk GAME BOY to the desert edges of the stadium.

REIKO: Hey. I heard you might have sparklers over here for sale?

CRENSHAW & LAMAR *[laughing at her]*: Sparklers. Heh-heh okay.

REIKO: Or firecrackers, I don't know.

CRENSHAW: No way on the crackers, kiddie.

REIKO: I feel like maybe sizzlin' something in uh open place.

CRENSHAW: You got permission to be in this sort of / league of …

REIKO: I hold my head up! Thought there might be sissy pellets on the ground I could play with out of consolation for my loser status up to now.

CRENSHAW: Sorry Lolly. 'Gainst the policy.

LAMAR: What sorta open place.

REIKO: I dunno, sometimes I feel a sparkle deep inside of me. And I want to let it, you know, show.

LAMAR: Iron on.

CRENSHAW: Scratch n' sniff.

They laugh beevus and butthead style

REIKO: I look at the sky on a pitch black night and I wish them real stars weren't really real.

CRENSHAW: What else would they be.

LAMAR: Them sorta stars…

REIKO: Maybe they're pre-frozen from a tricentennial that hasn't quite occurred yet. Maybe they're paused in the middle of some DVD kid wiz!! Til somebody comes along and—pulls our loyalty right out of us. In a strand of royal blue that's snappin' in the breeze. I think of loyalty as pretty much blue.

GAME BOY: And red's the masochism of it. Ain't it Lolly.

REIKO: Oh you can call me Lolly. I know I can't override the Lollies up to Texie status.

LAMAR & CRENSHAW & NARRATOR *[doubletake]:* Little Texie!? Hm.

NARRATOR: Hm.

REIKO: I keep tryin' but that bitch is set up in a loop and she'll always set me back. I'm no threat to her, some nameless outta nowhere kid, she knows that prong is stacked. Well anyway. I'll take my sparklers and be on my way. See you in the stadium tonight.

REIKO picks up sparklers, small explosion.

CRENSHAW: How you payin' for them sparklers, kiddo?

LAMAR: You know I'd stoop down to your level. But I'd be all balls and chin.

CRENSHAW: Fuck puppet.

LAMAR: On your mark.

TAKESHI #7: back of the bike: They start wrestling and grunting, giving REIKO a chance to get on the back of the SUPRAKNIEVEL bike and abscond with GAME BOY.

GAME BOY: Light your sparklers in a blind spot, Lolly. I'll pick up on that and save you from the sand box.

Scene 8. THE GREATER SILHOUETTE

Another prophecy from TEXIE. Triggers opening of stadium's protective roof to the actual warzone, also known by the cheatcode GdzillaX

NARRATOR: Goddam alliances. *[kinda mumbled]* If it IS for real. And this just in from the actual Little Texie in the sky, and laced with cheatcodes, yeah….We have deciphered the invisible ink, so yeah—Way to keep that bicentennial alive, Little Texie!

"Night Vision Goggles" by a Little Invisible Girl

You the pin prick

In the pin prick stars

Holding my delay

Toy eyes

Surround you

So you play

When the monstahs

Wrestle your explosion

Softly from the

Ground away

NARRATOR *[cont'd]*: Whoever thought our warriors would be five and so poetic! We've got that crypt decoded as "The Greater Silhouette is falling open and above you." The Greater Silhouette is falling open and above you.

She looks up. Black desert sky. Stars appear to twinkle.

NARRATOR: Hm. Go figure. It's a blackout.

NARRATOR seems confused for the first time in the game.

Hiwa Bourne undercover as a Lolly Girl (Theater of Note, LA)

Justin Brinsfield as Crenshaw and Jennifer Ann Evans as Lamar
(Theater of Note, LA)

Jonathan Klein as Game Boy/Supraknievel (Theater of Note, LA)

Hiwa Bourne as Lone Wolf Reiko (Theater of Note, LA)

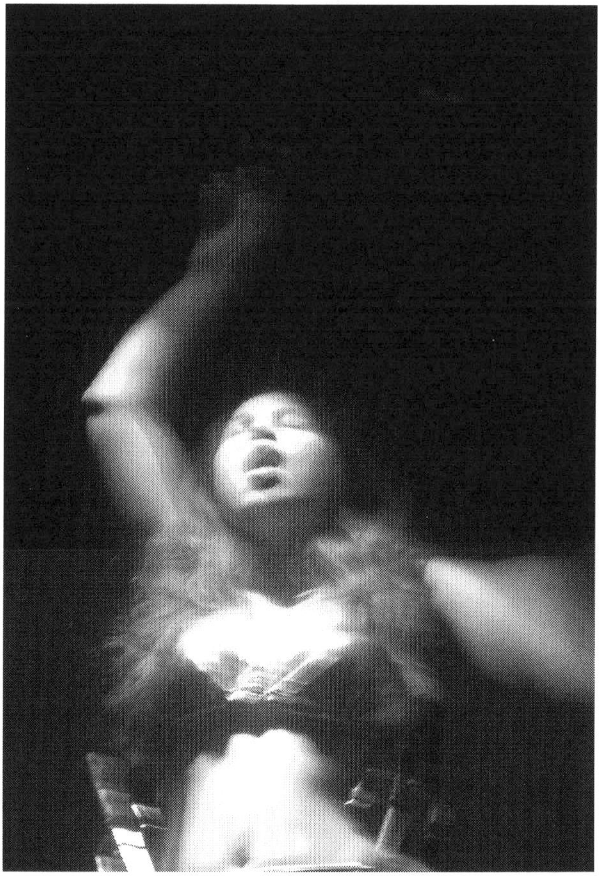

174 ~ *Stadium Devildare*

Costume Design: Joel Scher & Gray Creasy; Prop/Special Set Design: Gray Creasy, Rich Werner, Brian O'Conner Jenny Nissenson, Josh Mohr, Erin Brewster; Stadium Logo designs: David Croy

Scene 9. FUMBLING FINGERS AT THE DEADBOLT

TAKESHI #8: wrestle wrangle. REIKO lights her sparklers. GAME BOY appears. They wrestle softly on the ground.

GAME BOY: Lay still. I have the intel rolling for your search n'rescue.

REIKO: I can handle temperature. I can handle pestilence.

GAME BOY: You never been out here at night. They got night vision pivots on your consumer orbit, soon as you step off your track.

REIKO: When did I do that. I barely even thought about it.

GAME BOY: You think you hacked into the smartest little potholes. Well there's a few things to unravel, missy.

REIKO: Don't start with that or you'll get your precious engine tampered with. I can fire into plain sight where your most bestial foe is so-called hidden.

GAME BOY: Been fighting him my whole life, undercover, took the flag, the cross, what have you.

REIKO: Well I would hope so. If you're Evel Supraknievel.

"Alliance"

GAME BOY surrenders and REIKO camouflages the Suit of Guts'n'Glory.

GAME BOY: You know I'm just the stuntman piloting the Suit. But I've been following you for some time because I wanted you to be my witness when I finally, um, "surrender" my omnipotent wardrope to the desert.

REIKO: So you've heard about my great uncle's legacy.

GAME BOY: Okay. That's part of it. I xeroxed all his interviews, how he studied animals at the zoo. How he acted in the head of the original Godzilla from 1954-1972. Underwater sometimes with his students crouched behind him from the university. How it was hot as hell in there. Inside the monster's face. That it was very dark and lonely. Isolated. I thought you might relate to that.

REIKO: What makes you trust I won't take over all your "power" when I rip this Suit off of you?

GAME BOY: I trust there's somebody else who will do that. I think you know who's been pretending to let me win.

REIKO: Crenshaw has been marked when he came out here cocky. Now blows radioactive fire through multiple nostrils, which appear all over his body when he steps into sand. His victims explode in a lovely fireworks display.

GAME BOY: Probably gonna do that to the both of us after I get naked.

REIKO: He'll be picking up that scent of fear. By day, he uses prepubescent prowess. Which is lame. We gotta camouflage ourselves and your important game piece, which is something I can do for you.

GAME BOY: *[shaking like a leaf]* It's here surrounding us, derived from all that '70s exotic fabrication. I can feel it. Shit, I was playing that Suit too vintage anyway. I was a sitting fucking duck. Who knows who I'm embedded with at this point…

REIKO grabs him and throws him down almost stripped naked.

REIKO: What are you prepared to do now, Game Boy? To fall out of step with your tribe? To break rank? Incur some disapproval?

GAME BOY: That's really bleak—So which side did I choose. I'm sort of turned around here.

REIKO: Are you prepared to die? To murder?

GAME BOY: Okay, well/ okay…

REIKO: To commit acts of sabotage that may cause the death of innocents

GAME BOY: I guess I.

REIKO: To cheat, to forge, to blackmail, to corrupt the minds of children in the greater, future interests of your nation…

GAME BOY: *[catching on, dim memory of 1984]* I am prepared to cause addiction, prostitution, venereal disease, anything to demoralize or weaken the Regime—

REIKO: To lose your identity, to have no comrade, no encouragement. To get no help when you are finally busted. To live without hope and without results.

GAME BOY: I will work, I will be caught, I will confess and I will die. These are the only results that I will ever see.

REIKO & GAME BOY: There is no possibility that any perceptible change will happen within my lifetime.

REIKO lays the Supraknievel Suit down on an American flag.

REIKO: Let's go. It's camouflaged. They'll never find it here. It'll disintegrate more rapidly in this climate. You gotta get inside my parachute.

GAME BOY: You get to keep the parachute?

REIKO: It's also hidden in plain sight. Just get in.

Scene 10. BULLDOZE

The Dazzler brothers realize the lid is off the stadium and freak out.

"Blackout"

LAMAR: No way. No fucking way.

CRENSHAW: What's the cheatcode on the blackout?

LAMAR: Maybe treasure hunt for weapons and collect the pieces 'til you reach the final level, beat the game?

CRENSHAW: Don't think so. Perfect score is unachievable, you lose your weapons as you go.

LAMAR: Convention'ly guerilla, but more of a hatred than the kid that's workin' off his student loan.

CRENSHAW: One brother maybe buries his Amber Alerts deeper in the yard.

LAMAR: Gotta love that first pitch of the season.

CRENSHAW: Um I hate to say but I think I'm seeing real stars in this blackout.

LAMAR: No way. That little beast was right—she took the lid off the Stadium. That's the cheatcode on her greater silhouette… those are real stars, this whole bullshit game is live.

They freak out in the first few moments of a war zone still at night. TAKESHI ALARM SOUNDS.

CRENSHAW: I hear fucking roaring. Oh my god, it's like the veins of it are like exploding in its throat. Just like they said it would be if it's weapons grade. Oh my God. It's the alarm. I can't even fucking lift myself.

LAMAR: No show. The lovebirds have absconded.

CRENSHAW: Now's the time for you to kick in all that sideman bullshit, man. Let's see what happens when there's no No. 1 to sidle up to, bastard.

LAMAR: 'Cept for one important game piece. I had us tracking on the roaring. Look't this.

LAMAR finds Supraknievel Suit. CRENSHAW takes it. Turns against LAMAR.

CRENSHAW: Lemme have what's cumin' to me, brother.

TAKESHI #9: Assault. CRENSHAW beats LAMAR brutally to a bloody pulp.

NARRATOR: Congratulations. Brothers. On a clever twist of fate. I guess it's time for me to focus on your new achievement.

CRENSHAW [*starts getting dressed in Supraknievel Suit*]: Just wanna say to each potential American who wantsa dream the dream, if you can't feel me you're a threat to this regime.

NARRATOR: What does that mean? /To feel the—

CRENSHAW: Like-minded eyes connecting with my eye, double-clicking on my eye. Steal away to some dark loophole such as cash, handwriting, dial up or rotary—

NARRATOR: So you think this was an AM radio sort of a roaring that was used to forge/ this

CRENSHAW: Off the record/

NARRATOR: Right but captured by some Fisher Price pixelvision camera once marketed to kids under/ thuh-rrreeeeee

CRENSHAW: More than half the world is children now. We are reaching out to their convenience. Adjusting our realities to animate the target zone. The beasts of your first nightmares crouch in the crack of the door. Barbaric neighbors you must learn to dominate, expel, starve and humiliate.

NARRATOR: What neighbors are these—ssssssuddenly these neighbors??/ that we never heard of, suddenly we have to—

Joey Hood as Crenshaw (Rude Mechanicals, Austin)

"Bulldoze Rant"

CRENSHAW's acceptance speech

CRENSHAW as SUPRAKNIEVEL: Bulldoze the dependence, poverty, despair. Bulldoze the contaminated breeding of defected ones who can't survive, can't modernize, can't cooperate, can't organize. Bulldoze the casualties, the human errors, friendly fire, babies born with two heads one of which has parasitic nature, lips and teeth. Bulldoze the ones with nothing left to live for, no appreciation of their human rights, thoughts buried in the sand. Bulldoze the war crimes that we tampered with. Bulldoze the vengeance of the wounded soul. Bulldoze the collateral damage. Bulldoze the mechanized pain and megadeath. And then just syndicate the column in an endless insult, game of drivel. Staging point of no return. Too familiar for top story. Cauterize the gashes of the soul with seams of capital and high arousal kept in stimulation, static thrust, orgasm of the onward, and reality as porn, porn as reality, and kiddie porn as privatized for the naughty reach of every home computer. It's about the airborne blowing of shit up and perfect stunts and bulldoze!

NARRATOR: I'm a little stuck still in the question of these sudden neighbors.

CRENSHAW: Remix your footage and confusion. Create a story we can FOLLOW, westward ho, pretend to leak it, see what happens. If that's not compelling, then keep running it and running it until you reach that syndicated satisfaction. Of. The. BULLDOZE.

LAMAR: So you would hawk the Suit someday to foreign corporate interests?

CRENSHAW: Come on let's do the Superpower Syndrome. Everybody. Go. Drop down and feel your fucking superpower. No. 1, and number fucking one across the planet, in the world!

"Superpower Syndrome"

CRENSHAW does the superpower dance, and makes NARRATOR and LAMAR join in.

CRENSHAW: If you don't feel that coursing through your superpower blood than you are never gonna feel the pleasure of the bulldoze.

TAKESHI #10: zero sum. LAMAR takes CRENSHAW brutally out of the game

NARRATOR: And this just in from Texie, who would like to clarify the rules a little. In that, up 'til now, elimination meant just a rotation, shame in rank or scoring, yeah that's right, a realignment with each strategy performed. From now on Texie, yes, you must eliminate each other and no one really wins and no one CAN win—Is what I think they mean by zero sum. I think we mentioned that in passing, in case the tape gets rewound as an archeological piece of evidence. A sort of detonated propaganda as you all have been such lovely propaganda. There we go, we've got some missiles coming in, so I'll just wrap this up. Good luck to you.

LAMAR all but buries CRENSHAW alive.

LAMAR: You can feel it this way from beneath the shovel, buried in the pieces blown to mist in the blackout sand.

Scene 11. GDZILLAX

Radiation, plexiglass and bloodbath

Guerilla battlefield until the dawn breaks sky.

Scene 12. NIGHT PARACHUTE BATTALION

Report from the actual war zone. Involuntary signature weapons and casualties accruing...

"Shoulder Blades"

REIKO [*slightly airborne in partial parachute*]:

In my head, there are so many flashing levers, and a lurching feeling, like I'm plunging headlong on some wheel below, crushing entire cities under my wheel. It's like the feeling of a giant in a land of small and probably more mobile units, tiny feet or bloody claws much easier to hide. But I wanted to turn my attention, turn my...head to see you behind me. How my hair must be blowing wild without my helmet on. Maybe my hair is blowing into your eyes and mouth, if you don't have a helmet on, and you would be brushing it away, to see ahead... And then. *I feel that you are gone, but I still feel you.* Lifted in the smoke of weapons. Firing from my shoulders. Out of the tube into the air. Out of the tube and into the air. Heavy in the tube and lighter in the air. So many missiles coming right out of my shoulder blades. Snake or circle search and then a bulk charge from above me. As if it was flying. What I was attempting to destroy. But then it dawned on me that it was tall. It was very very tall.

"Like Nausea"

GAME BOY *[in partial parachute]:* Could there be a nightmare sort of sea like this? Under the sand? I mean I knew that there were wells you dig underground for, but this sort of ashen water with the oxygen burned out of it—and something like black rock, wet and curving, like volcanic ash that hardens—Something too sensitive inside my capacity to think without some message to be used as messaging device. I feel the acoustics of the codes floating through me in a sort of wave—correcting the kill patterns, detecting the vast, black rock that seems to move, and seems to walk into the classifying of it as something long ago forsaken by us, wasted or refused. I can feel the seams inside of it, that it has been improved. It has made itself more mobile in relation to its size. It's targeting in real time, as they say, deep reality. And then it detonates to change its passwords all to maybe Grand Copper Canyon 1984, an old plan for intercontinental range at hypersonic speeds that we abandoned for training in wooded areas or stormy weather. Like nausea I lunge toward it with a moored torpedo. Like nausea, I send my signals to burrow into its alarm, thinking "payload, misted fuel…" *I must find you again.* I want to take your weapons at the door and bathe you. I try to keep you sequestered in my mind so they won't find you when they read it. I encrypt all my memories of those few, rare moments in the horizon of my lifespan… my shelf life chewed open and spewed out in fire…

"Bang Harder Derby"

LAMAR: I am assembled into something familiar, tailored for my personality and skill. A closely fitted weapon that is welded shut so none of the door slat things can fly open on impact, which I grew up with really. No passengers, no glass, nothing loose that could shatter so just these sorts of goggle windows, but you don't see optically at this point. It's infrared or thermal or some dot that dances around, and you have signals that are coded so you can't get jammed. And then you just like track the target super fast and ram into it really hard just like those old BANG HARDER Derby T-shirts. And I call the payloads that are gonna squeeze out in the impact "Orange Crush" because of that one soda that never seemed to go anywhere but ended up in Mexico, hot and flat like the pulp of all these soft, soft targets. And in between the demolitions I just build my breaker wall and hope the great big monster pillars don't waddle onto my little trench. I really think of it as driving in a car when I get out here. Like I'm just hot rodding it at speeds of mach 5 or 7 into its scales, where I'm sure the seeds of populations that tried to glom on—are still burrowed down in there. And then I feel one of the crashes that comes all the way inside my armor fix. I see the edge of something tearing into me. A sort of bruising blood that rolls around you when you're in a bad collision. And I know this is a really bad collision.

Epilogue. NOH ROYALE

GAME BOY and REIKO opt out of the game they're winning in the only way they can in a spare and white void. Narrator becomes a Waki, her voice distant like an AM Radio

NARRATOR as WAKI: Wedding dreams that flash before a child laying down. Small fumbling fingers at the deadbolt...

GAME BOY has a bouquet of blossoms waiting for REIKO behind the door and lets her in. He takes her weapons then he lays her weapons down.

REIKO: We can't keep winning.

GAME BOY: Can't command it from inside the monster's face

REIKO: So then the time has come to lay our weapons down.

GAME BOY: I'd like permission to die with you, Reiko, tonight.

REIKO: Only if I go first. You can change your mind. I'll never know, don't worry. And if we lay here in this blasted house forever. I think the walls'll grow back from the holes.

GAME BOY: Come on and take my weapons at the door.

REIKO: Game Boy.

GAME BOY: Silly.

REIKO: Let's get undressed in the radio.

GAME BOY: Too bad we're not exactly national enough to leave behind some shadows getting old and paired across the morning, sleeve to sleeve.

NARRATOR: Toy Tea...

They drink toy tea with formal ritual movements.

REIKO: I'm just, I'm sorry I get so upset. Beyond this one survival possible, there's pretty much a damp splash of some vomit in the end and, yeah some sudden F/X, in like, in the absent chair. A grey kid I was friends with in between the desk legs. Sneakers soaked in fuckin' blood. Some cute girl, crumpled in a sad look bending over.

GAME BOY: It's a problem that I can't defragment. Can't delete the ...cautionary...old-time bugle.

NARRATOR: Warm Bath *[they bathe each other]*

REIKO: I wish I had my diary to burn.

GAME BOY: Come in from the program.

REIKO: Press you to the floor still in my camouflage.

GAME BOY: No clutter in the house. No filth.

REIKO: Your fingers fumble at the lock to let me in. We're the crosshairs, but it's just me.

GAME BOY: Let me in.

REIKO: Oh it's you.

GAME BOY: Come in.

REIKO: Take my sword please.

GAME BOY: Okay, your sword is heavier tonight. Okay.

REIKO: Should I make up some tea for us?

GAME BOY: No. We'll take a bath and lay down then I'll shave my death face. You can paint your eyes and put on your kimono.

REIKO: Will you look at my whole body in the lamp one last time.

GAME BOY: I'll wait for you on the bed to come out of your bath.

NARRATOR: Touching Up Her Pokemon—she looks even younger. Cruel radio...split like a knap sack east to west. And barely brushed with trembling. Tighten up the sabre hilt.

REIKO: No glory. We leave behind no flag, no nation, no house, patriots none beyond the two.

NARRATOR: They make love on the battlefield that has no glory.

GAME BOY: It's the same rosette of fingers that you had before. This afternoon when you came back. Clustered fingers, buds of spring, to splay your fine determination

NARRATOR: Rosette—She holds her sword

REIKO: As I prepare to sit cross-legged. And undo my brass buttons. My blood, oh my blood is welling up. There is a sharp cry of the future in my ears. I need an effort in the blow. I'm waiting for that molten chaos sort of feeling to kick in, prisoner in a cage of pain

GAME BOY: Um, maybe we should do this more together. I mean at the same time...I can't stand to think of sloshing through your warm blood and preparing myself after you...Let's just put our hands together and maybe lunge up in the air beyond some cliff with the sea in the background.

REIKO: Okay. But you have to say your last words also.

GAME BOY: I don't have much to say. I was hoping maybe I'd face west and you'd face east so we could look like a double-headed dragon. That's why my screenname is Palaiologoi because of Asia Minor getting ruined at Constantinople but maybe someday getting back together.

REIKO: Maybe we can write that on a note.

GAME BOY: Nah, let's just forget it and go back out on the death ground. Fight to the end.

REIKO: Let me try it again and you just follow me, okay. We'll lay down in the furthest edges of the game.

GAME BOY: Game Girl.

NARRATOR: Game.

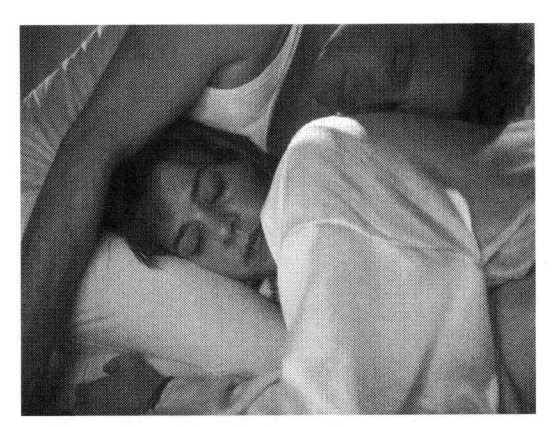

Lana Lesley and Jason Liebrecht (Rude Mechanicals)

~ END OF STADIUM ~

194 ~ *Stadium Devildare*

Afterword

By Randy Gener

People often take their cues from the attention-grabbing subtitles of Ruth Margraff's operas and plays. In a review or interview, a critic will invariably attempt to decode the extensions Margraff adds to her suggestive titles. What might be the implications of the playwright's billing of RED FROGS as "a burlesque mirror for the summer purgatorio" or of her dubbing THE ELEKTRA FUGUES (memorably) as "a black box recording of classic disaster"? Are these subtitles declaring something beyond what is already expressed in the titles? It is almost a game, this need to sleuth around for insight in the baroque verbal turns of these subtitles. At one point an interviewer from *American Theater* magazine pointedly asks Margraff, "Are you reluctant to characterize your work as plays?" When she responds that the subtitles point to the forms she is exploring in a particular piece, she provokes people to go hunting. We can't help but take the bait.

Sometimes, as in the case of STADIUM DEVILDARE: "Battle for Gdzilla X," however, the subtitle trucks in a major allegorical plot point. Instead of characterizing the play's form or yielding instant clarity, it adds a new layer of description. It might serve as a semi-title in its own right. For the Los Angeles production of STADIUM DEVILDARE, someone had the helpful idea of slapping on scrappy ad-like copy — "A new reality program for the American arena" and "A tale of future sport...America to the extreme" — to isolate new levels of illumination about the play's reality-TV game-show format in which four warrior-contestants in action-ready costumes compete against one another for the honor of ultimately facing an actual war zone, known by the code "Gdzilla X" while dressed in the supernaturally powered jumpsuit of Evel Knievel.

One of America's most formally adventurous playwrights, Margraff invests each new work with fresh stylistic inventions. The strange poetry of her work kicks up a rush of words and images and music that exhilarate, stimulate and disorient. Sometimes, it might seem to be too much. Then again, we are used to encountering a majority of writing for the stage that is prosaic and ordinary. Most plays don't work on you like Margraff's melodic language does. They don't stay with you long after the performance, as Margraff's dream-like visions do. Her plays — some of which she has mischievously dubbed "electric and hysteric operettas with punk bands" or "extended barroom brawls" or "martial-arts operas" or "gypsy operas for troubadours" — might be harbingers of brand-new genres. For readers, the subtitles come off the page as riffs. For actors, directors and designers who wish to stage them, they function more like stage directions that you would be a fool to ignore; they sum up the very lively qualities that make the poetic landscape of her scripts breathe and live on stage. They are instructions for breathing.

Margraff often works collaboratively with other artists. As can be gleaned from the production histories of the three plays collected in this book, her early works were made to order for a number of experimental ensembles in the music-theater Petri dishes of New York City, Los Angeles and Austin, Texas. Her colleagues — a striking number of them musicians and composers — would hand her disparate ingredients, and her job was to pull things together and concoct rich stews. Her plays therefore demand audiences who are prepared to go where unpredictable minds might wander — theatergoers who are able to enjoy what she calls the "emotional vibrato" of a spoken text or who delight in the spectacle of outrageously staged encounters.

Margraff has been labeled a language playwright, and she shares Gertrude Stein's partiality for a language in which "words have the liveliness of being constantly chosen." Margraff's work cherishes fevered poetry, aggressive comedy, contradiction, density, the changeability of a character, cascades of high and low cultural mashups, and a ruthless critique of society and politics. Her plays defy easy summary. Even when they remake the Greek classics, their plots are not readily discernible. Her characters are always vying with one another. The pairs of lovers and patriotic brothers of STADIUM DEVILDARE lust for victory and fight for supremacy. The rowdy Coney Island working girls of RED FROGS stage a coup against the queen of all media at her summer home in Nantucket. The mythic characters of THE ELEKTRA FUGUES, Margraff's first opera, are locked in a battle that is as personal as it is acoustic. As Margraff writes in an introduction to the published script in *Divine Fire: Eight Contemporary Plays Inspired By The Greeks*, "*I fell in love with various definitions of 'cadence' as a way of writing character and the idea of a 'fugue' as a way of translating disaster. I started drawing some of my characters' cadences onto music paper and realized that Elektra's rage might be at the heart of the fugues of her family's catastrophe, if you listen to her rants as a pitch to which her family's voices adjusted in counterpoint.*"

Like Stein and Tennessee Williams, both of whom reanimated language, Margraff begs us to share with her, in each of the three plays of this collection, her own sense of discovery. The blends and sounds of these plays make them more like collages than narratives. On page and in performance, they look sculpted, scored and built. The themes they tackle and their combination of cultural influences represent familiar places (Coney Island, Nantucket or ancient Greece), but they also suggest some more profound configurations — a more politicized arrangement of experience. Take the two classically inspired plays. Unlike Sophocles' version, THE ELEKTRA FUGUES doesn't just have one lucid moment of recognition between the black-clad Elektra and her long lost brother Orestes — it's got five such recognition scenes, each one amping up the tension and raising the dramatic stakes. Margraff also grafts into the ancient legend the character of a gently befuddled Oxford academic Gilbert Murray, a passionate scholar and translator from the 1930s who yearns to be somehow united to the grief-stricken heroine. RED FROGS takes its inspiration from Aristophanes' FROGS, but it also throws into the pot satirical helpings of Karl Marx's teachings, Dante's DIVINE COMEDY and Charlie Chaplin's slapstick moves. More importantly, this play bites off the big questions. Margraff takes on class, sex, pop culture, media mendacity and the patriarchal Old Left, scoring points by using a performance style that is shamelessly burlesque.

Margraff's ornate work has invited charges of being obfuscating, opaque or pretentious. After returning from a trip to India in 2009, she wrote an essay for *The Drama Review* entitled *"Toward a Neo-Cubist Alamkara Movement in a Reality-Programmed Theatre Near You."* As artistic manifestos go, the ideas and non-sequiturs she packs into that essay are provocative and heavy-duty. Not only she does she come out of the avant-garde closet by announcing that her plays are "neo-Cubist" in manner, she also draws an explicit connection between her work and the Sanskrit notion of "alamkara." *"It means 'enoughmaking' or an ideal ornamentation,"* she writes, *"and comes from a Hindu belief that 'unadorned is not enough' and that any doorway or dress or margin of a manuscript has to be embellished to be truly pure because it is incomplete unless it overflows with florid decoration and metaphor."*

Margraff argues that writers should not be ashamed of adorning their language with metaphor. A poet's tongue may be the last taboo, but it can be our best defense against the daily counterfeits of mediated talk and the corruptions of ideological propaganda with which our overly politicized culture constantly barrages us. In an interview she recently gave me for *IATC: CRITICAL STAGES Revue de l'AICT Issue 5*, Margraff explains:

> "Most U.S. narratives depict characters that struggle with class conflicts, but they won't directly address class as a central issue, because most of our theatre's audiences belong to the upper-middle class, and they are worried about losing their status: the fragile status of being in the know, of being in the audience to begin with. Most theatre artists also come from the upper-middle class or have to make their way there eventually to stay in business. Or they have to write for and serve that upper-middle class audience. This condition is the glass ceiling dramatized in my play RED FROGS. This is the reality program of STADIUM DEVILDARE. And it finds its roots in the dysfunctional family of THE ELEKTRA FUGUES.

America waged wars, because we were duped by language. America couldn't read the lips of George W. Bush and Dick Cheney and their corporate cronies. We are involved now in class warfare, of which Occupy Wall Street is one manifestation, because we can't understand the onslaught of language hitting us like a typhoon everyday about who we are supposed to be and what we are supposed to buy. We are duped as to what class we really are. The wealthy people do photo ops as if they were one of us—if we only had more confidence. The poor vote as if they are rich. All three of these plays (RED FROGS, THE ELEKTRA FUGUES and STADIUM DEVILDARE) tackle violence, class and language in some way. ELEKTRA FUGUES is embroiled in a war that erupts from a tonal pitch of dissent and truth. RED FROGS teems with over-the-counter girls who try to ignite a revolution based on Marxist poetics but end up weeded out and hogtied by the torso of it and thrown back out into the sea. STADIUM DEVILDARE reimagines the Iraq war as a reality program on the verge of syndication. My most radical gesture in these works is the poetry in which I choose to traffic. I have been saying for a while now that form is more radical than content. What we fear most is that reality is in any way formless."

Margraff is allergic to the tenets of American realism and conventional dramaturgy. At the same time, she brings to bear an Eastern European musicality to her whitetrash Americana characters. Inspired by Greek blues and Balkan Roma gypsy music, Margraff refers to her recent work as world folk opera. Her plays are remarkable for their rhythmic cadence — for their irrevocable sense of song. When she writes plays without music, she works tirelessly to concoct a kind of lyric theater in which she freely delineates her operatic obsessions. As Margraff states (once again from TDR): "If I had to draw what I think language could sound like now in the throes of writing plays that have become less like plays and more like music, I would see language in cubist layers of color, brushstroke, and texture."

Elsewhere in that same TDR essay, Margraff remarks: "I yearn like hell for a cubist tremor in the theatre, in the voice, in space and time." Most people will probably put the stress on the word "cubist" over "tremor" —which would be a shame. It is too easy to praise Ruth Margraff for her formal qualities. Her plays feel so bracing that you want to commend them simply for being off the beaten track. Such a cool regard of her body of work, however, will not cut it. Ultimately this is too limiting an approach, and too narrow a critical view. The tremor that trembles in Margraff's work issues from the invigorating ferocity and high-pitched passions that propel her characters forward.

After you read these plays, it is actually better to pull back and look at them from afar. At a slight distance, you will see that Margraff is a landscape playwright whose ability lies in making plays more bizarre than real life. She cloaks her characters in exaggeration and a torrent of arias for the sheer pleasure of stripping them bare. And from the same distance, you will find that there is a reason for her rebellious streak as a playwright. In one way or another, the three plays that make up this book are tales of revenge. This narrative trope unifies them — it's what makes them all of a piece. Underneath the gaudy-farcical architecture of RED FROGS, beyond the contorted dysfunctional archetypes of THE ELEKTRA FUGUES and after the imperial games of violence in STADIUM DEVILDARE are over, Margraff's angry, trash-talking, live-wire characters are most impressive for their often overlooked emotional stature. They yearn like hell for moments of beauty and grace, and, as evinced by these two lovers in the final movement of STADIUM DEVILDARE, they display a much greater tenacity than the reality-programmed theater near you:

> REIKO: Will you look at my whole body in the lamp one last time.
>
> GAME BOY: I'll wait for you on the bed to come out of your bath.
>
> NARRATOR: Touching Up Her Pokemon - she looks even younger. Cruel radio...split like a knap sack east to west.
>
> REIKO: We leave behind no flag, no house, no nation, patriots none beyond the two.
>
> NARRATOR: They make love on the battlefield that has no glory.

Randy Gener is a New York City-based Nathan Award-winning editor, writer, critic and conceptual artist. A 2003 *New York Times* critic fellow, Gener serves on the editorial board and is the U.S. editor of *Critical Stages* (criticalstages.org), the webjournal of International Association of Theater Critics. He is the Broadway editor of *New York Theatre Wire* (nytheatre-wire.org), a site he co-founded in 1996. For his editorial work and critical essays as contributing writer and senior editor of *American Theatre* magazine, Gener received the George Jean Nathan Award for Dramatic Criticism, the Deadline Club Award for Best Arts Reporting from the New York chapter of the Society of Professional Journalists, five travel media awards for writing excellence from North American Travel Journalists Association Awards competition; and NLGJA Journalist of the Year, among others.

About the Author:

Ruth Margraff has been called a leader in the new opera movement in America and has toured with her CAFÉ ANTARSIA ENSEMBLE and other plays throughout the USA, UK, Canada, France, Russia, Romania, Serbia, Hungary, Italy, Greece, Turkey, Slovenia, Czech Republic, Croatia, Japan, Egypt, India, Azerbaijan. Her other writings are published by *Dramatists Play Service, American Theatre, Theater Forum, Performing Arts Journal, Playscripts, Inc., Kendall/Hunt, TDR, Conjunctions, New Village Press, Autonomedia, Skyhorse/Teatra V!da, Innova Records...* Ruth's recent writing includes ANGER/FLY for Trap Door Theater, critically acclaimed by Chicago press in 2012; SEVEN introduced by Hillary Clinton at the Hudson Theater featuring Meryl Streep for Tina Brown's Daily Beast summit currently touring the world; five martial arts operas with composer Fred Ho for the Apollo, Guggenheim, Brooklyn Academy of Music, etc.; THREE GRACES for the Ice Factory Festival (NYC,) Project X/CentralTrak Gallery (Dallas), Pivot Arts Festival (Chicago), and a forthcoming Ta'ziyeh passion play for Link's Hall/Shapiro/San Jose Stage Co. She's been awarded four Rockefeller Foundation commissions, two McKnights, Jerome Fellowship, NEA/TCG playwriting residency, two NYSCA awards, a Fulbright new opera fellowship and Illinois Arts Council Artist Project award among others and is alumna of New Dramatists, member of League of Professional Theater Women, Theatre Without Borders and has taught playwriting at Yale School of Drama, Brown University, UTAustin/Michener Ctr and is Associate Professor at the School of the Art Institute of Chicago. www.RuthMargraff.com

Special thanks to CentralTrak Gallery (Dallas, TX) artist residency for providing space and time for the editing of this book Dec-Jan 2012.

NoPassport

No Passport is a Pan-American theatre alliance & press devoted to live, virtual and print action, advocacy, and change toward the fostering of cross-cultural diversity in the arts with an emphasis on the embrace of the hemispheric spirit in US Latina/o and Latin-American theatre-making.

www.nopassport.org

NoPassport Press' Theatre & Performance PlayTexts Series and its Dreaming the Americas Series promotes new writing for the stage, texts on theory and practice, and theatrical translations.

Series Editors: Randy Gener, Jorge Huerta, Mead K. Hunter, Otis Ramsey-Zoe, Stephen Squibb, and Caridad Svich (founding editor).

Advisory Board: Daniel Banks, Amparo Garcia-Crow, Maria M. Delgado, Elana Greenfield, Christina Marin, Antonio Ocampo-Guzman, Sarah Cameron Sunde, Saviana Stanescu, Tamara Und

NoPassport is a sponsored project of Fractured Atlas, a non-profit arts service organization. Contributions in behalf of [Caridad Svich & NoPassport] may be made payable to Fractured Atlas and are tax-deductible to the extent permitted by law. For online donations go directly to https://www.fracturedatlas.org/donate/2623

BACK COVER:

Baltazar Castillo's Painting No. 5 "tired of the sacrifices (for Iphigenia)" is from his 2010 Sequence Series

mixed media: acrylic, feathers on canvas

The Sequence Series consisted of twelve works in two different sizes. When exhibited, in two rows, the works were meant to be approached left to right and followed a line that ran through eight of the rectangular works - down then left to right again. Four particular works (in square formats) were placed in the sequence as a pause from the rectangular movement of the others. The pause interrupted the line and contained a departure from the line into shapes of color, bursts of scraping, fragments of illusions, landscapes etc. and then picked up with the simple line again. Sometimes in painting the pause and development from the square format violated the rectangular ones.

www.baltazarcastillo.com

Made in the USA
Coppell, TX
09 January 2020